NightBorn

Some dreams must be set free.
Nightmares, after all, are still dreams.

NightBorn

A debut novel by

Theresa Cheung

6TH
BOOKS

London, UK
Washington, DC, USA

CollectiveInk

First published by Sixth Books, 2025
Sixth Books is an imprint of Collective Ink Ltd.,
Unit 11, Shepperton House, 89 Shepperton Road, London, N1 3DF
office@collectiveinkbooks.com
www.collectiveinkbooks.com
www.6th-books.com

For distributor details and how to order please visit the 'Ordering' section on our website.

Text copyright: Theresa Cheung 2025

ISBN: 978 1 917704 45 8
978 1 917704 46 5 (ebook)
Library of Congress Control Number: 2025935895

A CIP catalogue record for this book is available from the British Library.

Design: Lapiz Digital Services

UK: Printed and bound by CPI Group (UK) Ltd, Croydon, CR0 4YY
Printed in North America by CPI GPS partners

The manufacturer's authorised representative in the EU for product safety is:
eucomply OÜ - Pärnu mnt 139b-14, 11317 Tallinn, Estonia,
hello@eucompliancepartner.com,
www.eucompliancepartner.com

We operate a distinctive and ethical publishing philosophy in all areas of our business, from our global network of authors to production and worldwide distribution.

For all those who dare to believe in the power of their dreams

The dream is the small hidden door in the deepest and most inner sanctum of the soul.

—Carl Jung

Prologue

Alice saw the wave. It was a beast.

It rose slowly at first, the way a predator prepares to strike — silent, inevitable. It quickly gained speed, swelling into a towering monster, a force of nature, as if the ocean itself had decided to swallow her whole. The wave surged, easily 30 feet high, dark and roaring with a ferocity she could feel in her bones. It moved toward her with the relentlessness of fate.

She turned, panic seizing her as she raced up the beach, her bare feet slipping in the wet sand. The ocean was closing in — the world was closing in on her. Her breath came in jagged gasps, but the wave, too quick, slammed into her, yanking her under.

Her body twisted through the water, eyes stinging, lungs burning, desperate for air, clawing at the debris swirling around her — plastic, broken wood, seaweed, dead fish — but there was no solid ground to cling to. The current pulled her deeper, its grip tightening like cold fingers around her throat.

She gasped for air, choking on the water, the world a dark, crushing void. She couldn't see. Every nerve in her body screamed for release, but the ocean kept pulling, tumbling her in every direction, turning her body like a puppet with broken strings. She was drowning. No — *she was going to die.*

Something in her snapped.

Her feet hit something solid. Hard. Stone? She couldn't tell. All she knew was that she had to rise. She shoved upward, throwing her weight toward the surface with every ounce of strength she had left. Her body screamed, but she pushed harder, until her head broke through to air. For one split second, she inhaled — but the water dragged her down again, relentless, hungry for her life. She fought the instinct to panic.

She couldn't let it win. Not today.

Just breathe. Just breathe, Alice. Instinctively she let herself float, stilling her body, letting the sea carry her, accepting the weight of the water around her. She couldn't fight it anymore— but maybe she didn't have to.

Her feet found solid ground again. She *shoved* upward, defiant, gasping as she broke through. Sunlight blinded her.

Alice jerked awake, the sharp taste of salt lingering on her tongue, her body tangled in the sheets. The echo of the wave still thundered in her ears. The sunlight slanted through the bedroom window, blinding. Her pulse thrummed in her neck as if the sea still had its grip on her.

"You're okay. You're okay. It was a dream. Just a nightmare."

What if it wasn't just a nightmare?

Swinging her legs over the edge of the bed, Alice's feet hit the cold floor. *Had Swiss psychiatrist and dream analysis pioneer, Carl Jung ever felt this unsettled after one of his dreams? Had his own night visions ever made him question his grasp on reality?*

Her eyes flickered to the bedside table and her Red Book: the dream journal she'd named after Jung's own. Ever since she was young, she'd written down her dreams. But this one felt radically different from the rest.

It was too real, though it clearly wasn't literal. She lived more than an hour from the nearest beach and had never been to it. Was the dream a symbolic glimpse into her own future? A warning? Or something darker, deeper?

It was just a dream. Maybe it was just all the energy she'd poured into teaching Jungian dream analysis spilling out cathartically in a nightmare.

The feeling of drowning clung to her.

She grabbed her journal and scribbled out every detail of the dream. The ocean. The wave. The suffocating terror. Jung had called the act of recording dreams an act of self-analysis—so why did this one feel more like a clear and present danger than an analysis? Was it the forbidden mystery Jung had hinted at in his *Red Book*—that thin line between genius and insanity where revelation could be found?

Was her obsession with dreams driving her mad?

It was her calling, her passion. Perhaps, as director of the new program in Jungian Studies at the University of Central Florida, she could teach her students what she had dreamt and encourage them to analyze it; maybe it would be cathartic for them and for her.

What if her students were the key to unlocking the deeper meanings of her own dream? She could see herself standing before the class, scrawling on the blackboard, her voice filled with energy as she taught them about using their dreams to peer into possible futures, even to shape reality. *Inception*—she would reference that for sure, the perfect movie fix to illustrate how the subconscious could manipulate perception and even reality. What better way to introduce her students to the power of their own dreaming minds?

Alice pushed herself out of bed as the sinking feeling of the dream still clung tight. Blinking rapidly in front of her bedroom mirror, she forced herself to take deep breaths. Her long dark hair framing the mismatched eyes staring right back at her: one blue, one brown. She had always hated this difference. Always hidden it behind a pair of blue lenses.

A perfect illusion of normalcy, her blue lenses. They always worked—ever since she was 14, when her mother had taken her to the ophthalmologist to prevent the cruel teasing at school. Alice slipped them on, as though the simple act could shield her from her nightmare.

The rhythm of her repeated blinking to help the lenses settle helped bring a semblance of calm.

Something was coming, though; she could feel it. Something was drawing her, pulling her into the unknown. *Could she rise above and survive it?*

Alice dressed the part for her day ahead and stepped out into the bright light of the day.

Was the drowning nightmare a message? A warning? And if so, a warning about what?

Part One

Nightfall

The persona is a complicated system of relations between the individual consciousness and society, fittingly enough a kind of mask, designed on the one hand to make a definite impression upon others, and, on the other, to conceal the true nature of the individual.

—Carl Jung

Chapter 1

Alice's modest apartment was just a 15-minute drive from the sprawling campus in east Orlando, a vast 1,400 acres of land. Much of the land remained untouched, with wooded areas permeated by numerous jogging and hiking trails. She found a vacant spot in the faculty parking area, slung her bag over her shoulder and headed toward the stunning three-story building that housed the psychology and philosophy departments. They shared the massive building—74,250 square feet—with the Learning Institute for Elders, LIFE, which served seniors in the community.

By the time she'd graduated from grad school ten years ago, she'd been offered positions at the University of Miami, the University of Florida in Gainesville and here at UCF. The only place she could imagine herself living and working was Orlando, the home to Disney's "land of dreams," so here she had been since her first year in 2022, when Covid was waning. Mostly virtual classes that year. By early 2023, though, the shift to in-person learning again was complete, and she'd settled into the rhythm and rigmarole of campus life forever after.

Inside the lobby, she made her way through the throngs of students changing classes. One of her colleagues, Amira Mensa, a philosophy and communication professor, fell into step beside her as she made her way to her lecture hall. The two had instantly connected when they joined the university teaching faculty on the same day, and in the years that followed, they grew ever closer, bonding over their love for inspiring their students and their shared passion for coffee shops, antique bookstores and *The Lord of the Rings* trilogy.

"Hey, Alice," Amira called out. "You're not going to believe this."

Amira was a tall woman, about five ten to Alice's five four, so Alice often found herself craning her neck to meet her gaze.

Today, the sunlight streamed through the faculty's great glass windows and danced on the brightly colored beads woven into Amira's thick braided raven hair. Like Alice, she was in her late thirties, but her skin was tawny, not pale like Alice's, and her celadon eyes shone so vividly that sometimes Alice could almost glimpse her own reflection in them.

"Odd campus gossip?" Alice replied.

Amira's smile faltered. "It was *stranger* than that." Leaning in, "you were in my dream last night. But not like you think."

"What kind of dream are we talking about? Should I be flattered, or worried?" Alice tried a teasing British accent: "Was I the beacon of light guiding you through darkness? A savior when all hope had crumbled?"

Amira looked like the dream was still haunting her. "It started in my house—but not like any house I know. I found this room—hidden, buried behind a false wall. I didn't even know it was there. When I stepped inside, it was empty at first—just cold walls and silence. But then... *you* appeared." She paused. "It was you, but not all of you. Just your face, floating in the ether, like a creepy clown's face balloon. It felt *wrong*. Your hair was the same, but shorter—just at your ears—and it looked like you, every detail, every contour. But your eyes..."

Amira had never seen Alice without her blue contacts.

Amira shuddered. "One was dark, deep, like a void. The other was blue, bright, almost *alive*. There was something about them—something *wild*—like they weren't even *your* eyes anymore. And they were *watching*, always watching me, so intensely... it was chilling."

"An unfamiliar or secret or unused room is super—exciting news!" Alice blurted. She could never resist slipping into Jungian dream analysis mode. "Houses in dreams are typically a symbol of your sense of self."

Since her dreamwork research had become more widely acclaimed, Alice had lost count of the number of times her

4

colleagues and students shared their dream stories with her. She found it very moving; they didn't realize it, but they were baring something intimate, something hidden. Alice treated every interaction as sacred. And she always offered a positive spin, something that would help them.

"You might just be on the verge of something big, Amira — personal transformation is on the horizon, or needs to be. Hidden creative depths, unexplored potential — how exciting! But... but the room was empty until I showed up and took over. What was I doing?" Alice's voice dropped. "Was I drowning?"

"I don't know," Amira pondered. "You just appeared out of nowhere. And then the scene switched, and you were falling from the top of a cliff or something. You were disappearing into the darkness below. I stood at the edge, frozen, unsure — should I jump too, follow you down, or just watch as you vanished? I couldn't move. I just watched you fall, helpless, as the distance between us grew."

"Did I say anything as I fell?"

"Nothing."

"Interesting. Falling is the most common dream that people report — around the globe," Alice offered. "If I were your dream therapist — which, thank goodness, I am not, because the best person to interpret their dreams is always the dreamer herself, as dream symbols have personal as well as universal meanings — but if I *were* helping, I'd say the theme here is feeling unsupported. Or maybe even out of control." She didn't notice Amira wince. "The big question, though, is: Is this dream about you or about me? I'm still working on how to interpret the meaning of other people moonlighting in our dreams."

"Pray tell."

"Well, Jung believed that if the person in the dream is a family member or partner, it reflects your relationship with them. But if it is not an intimate relationship, they symbolize something about *you* — an aspect of your mindset or personality that you need to understand or integrate. Which means that when someone cameos in your dream it is like every other symbol in your dream: all about *you*. Think of a dream as stepping into a hall of mirrors revealing your unconscious mindset or beliefs. Dreams don't happen *to* you. They are created *for* you, by *you*, and they're *all about you*. That is their real magic. So, lecture over — which is it? When you think of me, what is the first word that comes to mind? Don't overthink it. Just look at me and go with what comes to mind."

"Perhaps this dream is about both of us heading for a fall? Aren't you always saying how much dreams love to pun? As for what springs to mind when I think of you, do you want brutal honesty, or should I go with what you might *want* to hear?"

"Honesty, of course," Alice declared. "Dreams don't lie, and neither should friends. What is the word? I promise I won't take offence."

Amira hesitated. "Incomplete."

The word caught Alice off guard. She loved it, though — dreams, like real friends, never hid the truth or offered up the predictable. No room for growth in what you already knew.

"Reflection — that's what dreams want us to do," she told Amira as they split off toward their respective classrooms. "Yours is already casting a spell on me. Let me know if you remember anything else about it, okay?"

She was like a dream vampire: never satisfied.

Of the 22 students in Alice's class — an ideal, not overwhelming number — only one had arrived so far. Neal King, a slender, brilliant kid with aspirations to be an artist, was sitting quietly at the back.

"Hey, Neal."

"Professor Sinclair." Neal shot to his feet, scooping up the project he'd been hunched over. "Got something I think you'll want to see."

He could barely contain his excitement as he lay a charcoal sketch on Alice's desk. It was a version of Alice—with shorter multicolored hair, a rounder chin, and eyes that mirrored her own blue lenses.

"This was you in my dream last night, Professor Sinclair. Only, one eye was blue, the other was brown. But I was out of brown chalk, so..."

Holy shit. Alice blinked. Slowly. "What was I doing?"

"We were discussing Jung—specifically, his first meeting with Freud, the whole telekinetic or mind-reading thing that happened when Jung asked Freud what he thought about the paranormal. I think we were talking about the movie version, but then for no reason you started throwing books at me and it freaked me out so much I woke up."

The Dangerous Method was one of Alice's films to reference to her students. "Viggo Mortenson as Freud and Michael Fassbender as Jung. Fascinating movie and dream referral to it, Neal. Shame about the book throwing, but perhaps that's just me telling you that my academic expectations of you are high."

Neal beamed. Other students began trickling in, chatting and settling into their seats.

Alice eyed the sketch. "Mind if I keep a copy of this?"

"Sure. But there's more," Neal said. "A couple of people in my comparative psyche class also dreamed about you— except for them it was more of a nightmare than a dream. Noah dreamt you buried him alive. Maybe he's struggling with his dissertation, feeling stuck? Eve told me you shot her with a pistol. Maybe she's feeling like forces outside her control are out to get her? Or she is just scared you might mark her down."

"Spoken like a budding Jungian dream analyst. But nightmares are still dreams, just extreme ones. Usually, the dreaming mind tries sending gentle messages first in dreams, but when we ignore them, things typically escalate into shock tactics. Nightmares can be tough to forget, which is exactly what your unconscious mind is always after: your undivided attention. When we dive into our shadow work seminars, you'll learn more about how nightmares expose what's repressed inside us, screaming for recognition—but which we refuse to face and understand in our waking time. So please," she glanced around at the small crowd gathering for class, "don't hate or be scared of your nightmares. Understand and communicate with them and have compassion for them, instead. Recognize them for what they are: transformative gifts to help you become wiser. They hold the key to your self-awareness and your personal growth."

Neal looked surprised.

"They are a warning light flashing at you from the inside out to show you that something about your current mindset isn't serving your best interests," she urged. "But that doesn't mean it is game over. You can change your perspective in a flash, steer a new course for yourself, if you want to stop waking up to a terrifying dream."

Salvador Dali had described his art as "photographs of his dreams." As Alice spoke, she could practically see the gears turning and imprinting themselves in Neal's head.

"I'm not sure if I should be flattered or freaked out by all these dreams starring me. It's next-level stuff, even for me. Did any of your friends mention the different-colored eyes as well?"

"They definitely did."

So, four people had dreamed about her last night. And Neal King's charcoal sketch bore an uncanny resemblance to her. But none of them had ever seen her without her contacts. What was any of it supposed to mean?

Class that day was a great session: a good vibe crackling. After, at the door, Neal handed her his sketch. "I did it on my iPhone too, in color, if you'd like me to send you that?"

"Wow," Alice said as the image appeared on her phone. It was her—eerily so. *Even the eyes.*

"Strange, huh?" Neal replied. "What do you think it means, Professor Sinclair?"

"No idea. For now, I'm chalking it up to a bizarre coincidence. In dreamland, would we expect anything less than the unexpected?"

According to Jung, coincidences were signposts, meaningful connections or synchronicities; they never happened without reason.

"Could it be something tapping into an archetype?" Neal questioned. "Something from the collective unconscious? People, things, feelings, the life stages we all share—just like you talked about today?"

"Guess we'll have to wait and see. But thank you again for the sketch. It's not every day you become the star in someone else's dream."

The employee dining room was always bathed in sunlight—owing to the row of tall windows. As usual, Alice and Amira had snagged one of the tables beside the copious amounts of glass so that they could watch the courtyard below. A fountain bubbled at its center, surrounded by a plethora of greenery and flowers that drew every bird in the neighborhood.

Today, someone had hung a couple of hummingbird feeders from the branches, and now a pair of these little beauties fluttered at the feeders, their tiny wings flapping ferociously in a near-invisible blur. Alice stared at the birds, sensing some message meant for her. Certain esoteric traditions and dream symbology treated birds as conduits between worlds: messengers, but only for the person who saw them.

Alice had never lost anyone she cared deeply about, so this wasn't a message igniting a fond memory of a departed loved one. Maybe it was an omen, a promise she'd soon make sense of this bizarre dream phenomenon.

The vibrant flowers before her were symbols of comfort and beauty, even hope. All Alice had to do was keep calm, rise above, and wait to see the bigger picture.

Amira looked to the hummingbirds fluttering at a feeder. "Wow, positive sign, those little guys," she slid into the chair across from Alice, setting her briefcase down and giving Alice a once-over. "You look like you've just discovered a major secret."

"Let's get some food first," Alice pleaded, "I'm starving."

Alice helped herself to a tuna casserole with mushrooms and cheese, a slice of warm, buttered French bread, and a glass of honey-flavored iced tea. The university cafeteria food was surprisingly good. Once they sat down again and settled in, Alice brought out her phone and showed Amira Neal's digital sketch. She passed it to Amira, who studied it so intensely that Alice had to consciously blink to keep her nerves in check.

"Wow, that really does look like you. Except for the different-colored eyes."

Making sure no one was watching; Alice took out her contact case and removed her contacts. When she looked up, Amira drew in a sharp breath.

"Christ. It really *is* you."

Quickly Alice popped the lenses back in. "Keep that to yourself, okay? My odd eyes have freaked people out my whole life. I'm only showing you because something strange is happening, and I need to find out what the hell is going on."

For several unraveling moments, neither of them spoke.

"This has 'Jung' written all over it," Amira finally broke the silence, "and not just because he's your absolute specialty. It reminds me of that story about his patient and the scarab. Total synchronicity—like life itself is pulling the strings."

In the fabled story, Jung was treating a woman who had recently dreamt of a golden scarab, an archetypal or universal symbol of death and transformation. At the exact moment she was telling him, a beetle tapped on Jung's window. He caught it and presented it to her. The incident had shattered her skepticism and opened her mind to therapy.

In a way, it had launched Jung's deep dive into synchronicity, even precognition.

Could the bizarre incident of people dreaming about her be the puzzle piece she'd been missing for her next big project? Alice had had an independent publisher hounding her for a book proposal ever since her TED talk on synchronicity, but she hadn't been sure of the direction she should take. Now her entire body hummed with the spark of possibility.

"You may be right," she told Amira, "but I need to dig deeper. You and Neal, and the other students, all know me. I'd be rattled if someone I've never met claims to have dreamed about me."

"Four people in one night is out there enough for me. It must mean something, don't you think?"

Alice's appetite left her. It felt as if the universe had just dropped a cryptic treasure map right in her lap—and the next step was all up to her. And what frightened her the most was not so much that she didn't have a clue about the how or why, but *what* she was dealing with.

By the time Alice left campus at around 4.30 that afternoon, no one else had approached her to tell her they had dreamt of her. Maybe it really was just a random fluke, one of those oddball blips in the scheme of things. She felt relief and a hint of disappointment in her reaction.

Jung would have seen that "blip" as a cosmic sign, a synchronicity, and run with it.

Why couldn't she?

Chapter 2

That night Alice lay in bed for what seemed like forever, wondering if tonight's dreams would bring more revelations. In the early hours of the morning, she woke with a start, but the sole remnant of her dreams was a tired cliché: her teeth falling out as she stood in her bathroom, trying to put her blue lenses in.

Not again. She scanned herself for hidden dream details. The dream was so familiar—it had recurred since her early teens—so she wasn't wasting precious sleep time jotting it down in her journal. Instead, she sank back into a dreamless sleep until her alarm nudged her awake.

She snatched up her mobile to search for a sign someone else had dreamt of her, but it was dead. *Fantastic.* She must've forgotten to charge it overnight. She took a few steadying breaths, letting the rising anxiety ebb. She threw on clothes, downed a quick breakfast, and headed out.

Ten minutes into her commute along the I-4, her phone—now plugged into the car charger—erupted in a cacophony of beeps, rings, and pings. Alarmed, Alice pulled off at the next exit— eyes peeled for a promise of gas, food, and some semblance of civilization. She parked at a pump, flexing her tense fingers before working up the nerve to check her phone.

Every dormant app Alice had signed up for but rarely found the inclination to post on had exploded. A digital avalanche crashing in from every angle, notifications popping up rapidly like hazard lights demanding her attention.

I saw a sketch of u on social media & it led me to u, your university email. Who the hell r u?

Don't have a clue who u r but why did I dream about you?

Professor Sinclair, you're the scary woman of my dreams, why? you are not even my type

News radio Orlando, here. Are you available for an interview?
WTF?

Someone had posted a sketch identical to the one Neal had drawn, asking: *Have you dreamed of this strange woman?*

And the replies kept on coming—students, colleagues, requests for interviews from Orlando's finest and not-so-finest media outlets, podcasts, magazines, websites. Dozens of strangers swore they'd dreamed of her too, comment after comment flooding in. Some even claimed she was pregnant in their visions.

That part almost made a twisted sense. Just a month ago, the hashtag #dreambabies had blown up, prompting a few fringe news channels to contact Alice for an expert take on what it meant to dream of pregnancy. She'd explained that it didn't automatically mean a real baby (unless the dreamer wanted one and was thinking about that potential in their waking life). More likely, it symbolized nurturing something new inside you, a creative project, or your inner child simply craving attention and nurturing.

She must have repeated the same line a thousand times: "Trust your intuition. Dreams are rarely literal. Focus on the symbolism. Go through all the metaphors for pregnancy. Look for that light-bulb moment, the meaning that clicks for you and creates a positive inner shift. That's the signal you have found the correct meaning of the dream for you."

Alice had spent years wishing dreams would catch the public's fascination and take the spotlight. Now here it was—unleashed in the most personal way possible.

How is my face in so many people's subconscious? And what does it mean?

Time seemed to freeze. Alice's mind flashed to all the years she'd championed dreamwork as a seriously neglected psychological self-help tool—lectured on how science still hadn't pinned down *why* we slept or dreamt. How dream recall correlated with better mental health, how missing the REM, or rapid-eye-movement, phase of sleep led to a spike in anxiety and depression. How it was proven that certain indigenous cultures that prioritized dreaming and taught their children how to understand and work with their dreams had reduced rates of crime and depression.

Alice had written countless blog posts and free interpretation resources, off-the-cuff dream interpretations she'd offered to anyone who asked. None of this could have prepared her for the waking reality before her now, front and center in other people's inner worlds, her own face stamped onto the dream lives of complete strangers.

Alice had spent years telling anyone who would listen that dreams spoke in a coded symbolic language—as nuanced and thought-provoking as the words of a poet or the brushstrokes of a painter. She'd urged people to interpret their dreams—their "night poetry"—in the same way they might tease out the meaning of what lay beneath the surface of a poem or painting. Dreams were an intuitive language, born from another state of consciousness. Decode the symbols personally, she said, and the hidden meanings would begin tumbling out.

Now all the research, lectures, articles about dreams she'd done felt like they were colliding in her mind all at once, a thousand dream voices roaring simultaneously in her head, all begging to be set free...

Abandonment: Do you feel neglected or unsupported in your waking life? *Accidents*: In what area of your life do you feel a loss of control? *Airplane*: Are you striving for higher goals or feeling a desire to escape? *Animals*: Are there basic instincts or emotions in your life that need attention? *Apocalypse:* Familiar ground shifting or a perspective change? *Babies*: Could this symbolize new beginnings or a need for care and protection? *Betrayal*: Is there someone or something you feel has let you down? *Birds:* Do you need to rise above and see the bigger picture? *Blood*: Could this represent loss, injury, or the need for healing? *Burglars*: Personal boundaries violated? *Cars*: Are you in control of your life or feeling directionless? *Celebrities/famous people:* Your desire for attention or to be noticed? *Being chased*: What are you running from/avoiding, and is it time to confront it? *Cheating/having an affair*: What are you cheating yourself out of? *Childhood*: Do you need to reconnect with your spontaneity or are you feeling in need of protection? *Climbing*: Are you trying to reach a goal or overcome an obstacle? *Clothes:* How do others perceive you? *Drowning*: Do you feel overwhelmed or out of control in some area of life? *Death*: Could this indicate an end, transformation, or fear of change? *Destruction*: Are you feeling threatened by forces beyond your control? *Exams*: Are you feeling tested or judged in your waking life? *Escape*: Is there something you're avoiding or trying to break free from? *Elevator*: Are you experiencing a rise or fall in your life circumstances? *Exam, feeling unprepared for it:* Feel tested or out of your depth? *Falling*: Do you fear losing control or fear failure? *Family:* What aspect of your relationship with them are they highlighting? *Fire*: Could it symbolize passion, danger, or the need to purge something in your life? *Fish:* Do you need to go with the flow, or as dreams love to pun does something look suspect or fishy? *Friends*: Are your relationships with friends causing you stress or joy? *Ghosts*: Are there unresolved issues from the past haunting you? *Gambling*: Are you taking risky decisions or seeking excitement? *Giant/Monsters*: Do you feel threatened by something large and powerful in your life? *Hiding*: Are you avoiding something or feeling insecure? *Hair*: Does your hair reflect your confidence, control, or self-image? *House*: Could the state of your house symbolize your mind or your personal life? *Injury*: Are you experiencing emotional or physical vulnerability? *Ice*: Are you feeling emotionally cold or detached from something? *Intruder*: Is someone or something invading your personal space or boundaries? *Impossible tasks/unable to complete simple tasks:* Do you always feel that others are ahead of you? *Job*: Is work causing stress or do you feel unfulfilled in your career? *Jealousy*:

Do you feel envious of others or insecure in relationships? *Jail*: Do you feel trapped, restricted, or confined by circumstances? *Killing*: Is there something or someone in your life you need to let go of? *Knives*: Are you feeling threatened, or is there a need for protection? *King/Queen*: Do you feel powerful, or are you grappling with authority? *Late*: FOMO and fear of not living up to expectations? *Lost*: Are you feeling directionless or uncertain about your future? *Lice/insects*: Are there small annoyances or irritations weighing on your mind? *Lifting*: Are you trying to overcome challenges or rise above difficulties? *Mobile phone (technology) malfunction*: Communication issues? *Monsters*: Are there overwhelming fears or challenges in your life? *Marriage*: Does this symbolize commitment, union, or a significant relationship? *Money*: Are you concerned with material wealth, security, or value? *Murder*: What forces outside your control are dictating how you feel? *Naked/nude/partially dressed*: Do you feel exposed, vulnerable, or unprepared for something in your life? *Nightmares*: Are you grappling with unresolved fears or anxieties? *Numbers*: Could numbers represent order, patterns, or something significant in your life? *Out of Control*: Do you feel powerless or overwhelmed by external forces? *Ocean*: Are you exploring your emotions or dealing with emotional depth? *Off Balance*: Are you struggling to find stability in your life? *People*: What aspect of your personality or mindset do they symbolize? *Plane*: Do you feel liberated or does this suggest your ambition is or needs to soar? *Pregnancy*: Is there something new in your life that requires nurturing and care? *Prison*: Are you feeling trapped, either by your own actions or by external factors? *Public Speaking*: Are you anxious about how others perceive you? *Quicksand or stuck in mud*: Do you feel stuck or sinking in a situation that's hard to escape? *Questions*: Are you seeking clarity or understanding in your waking life? *Quarrels*: Are you in conflict with someone or struggling with your emotions? *Rats*: Do you feel betrayed, or is there something unhealthy around you? *Running*: Are you avoiding something that you need to face? *Rain*: Could it represent cleansing, renewal, or emotional release? *Restroom, unable to find one:* Are you meeting your own emotional needs? *Secret room/treasure*: Untapped potential waiting to be unleased within you? *School:* Do lessons from your past still need to be learned? *Snakes*: Are there hidden threats, fears, or transformative forces in your life? *Space:* Do you need to open your mind to a fresh new perspective? *Spiders*: Are you feeling trapped, or do you need to address something slowly? *School*: Do you feel judged, or are you in a phase of learning and growth? *Teeth Falling Out*: Are you worried about your appearance, health, or feeling unassertive, that you haven't communicated your truth? *Theater:* Are you in the observer audience (passive) role or on stage playing your part? *Tornado*: Do you feel emotionally chaotic or threatened by an uncontrollable force? *Trapped*: Are you in a situation where you feel there's no escape? *Underwater*: Are you submerged in your emotions or feeling overwhelmed? *Unprepared*: Do you feel anxious about facing something you aren't ready for? *UFOs*: Are you encountering new, unknown, or unexplained elements in your life? *Vampires*: Do you feel drained, manipulated, or in need of energy rejuvenation? *Vacation*: Are you seeking a break, escape, or rejuvenation in your life? *Vehicles:* What direction is your life currently heading in and are you in the driver's seat or a passenger? *Victory*: Are you achieving your goals, or do you seek acknowledgment and success? *Water*: Are your emotions, both calm and turbulent, coming to the surface? *Wolves*: Do you feel protective, or is there an inner conflict between your instincts and social norms? *Weapons*: Are you feeling defensive or preparing for battle in your life? *X-rays*: Are you trying to see beneath the surface or gain insight into a hidden truth? *Xenophobia*: Do you fear the unknown or feel threatened by unfamiliar people or situations? *Yelling*: Are you feeling unheard or struggling to express your emotions? *Yellow*: Does the color yellow symbolize happiness, cowardice, caution or something unresolved? *Zombies*: Are you feeling disconnected, numb, or like you're just going through the motions? *Zero*: Does this symbolize a fresh start, a loss, or a sense of emptiness in your life?

"ENOUGH!"

Her head felt as though it would crack open under the sheer weight of it all. So many dreams were rooted in anxiety; people rarely came to her reporting visions of soaring midair like superheroes or dancing or meeting benevolent angels. *Good dreams, good life,* she'd always believed. But anxiety? That sadly seemed to be humanity's default.

She'd had these head-swimming episodes before. Only Luna, her medically prescribed comfort dog, could ease her through them, but Luna wasn't here right now, and this was the most brutal head crash ever. Maybe this was how a near-death experience felt: a rush of memory and energy, every thread of her life converging.

Had her feverish devotion to dreamwork somehow manifested this entire phenomenon?

She called the university, leaving a voicemail for her department head, Greta Hernandez. Alice needed to stay away from campus, at least for today, and spend quiet time with Luna.

Greta FaceTimed her back almost immediately. She sounded like she'd aged a decade overnight. "You're right to take a few days off. We've been slammed with calls since early morning — people demanding to know if this is some viral marketing stunt." A dramatic-looking redhead in her early fifties with two doctorates in psychology, Greta had a delicate Spanish accent and a brisk, no-nonsense air. "My daughter saw it all on social media and even asked if the department was staging some sort of psychology experiment, like that image was an ad for it."

Alice forced a laugh. "Is it?"

"Oh, absolutely," Greta snorted sarcastically, "something I cooked up during my morning run. Look, it's doing the rounds, so yes, it will get worse. But it will eventually blow over in a few days — that's how social media works. Take as much time as you need, a few days, a week. I'll find a sub for your classes and do a holding post saying it is just a coincidence that the online image looks rather like you."

Alice thanked Greta, promising to stay in touch. Swallowing a couple of painkillers handily stored in her glovebox as if they had been waiting for an occasion such as this, she pulled back onto I-4 and headed back home.

Alice's neighborhood was old, lined with cobblestone streets that dipped beneath the shady canopies of the towering oaks above. As she passed the sprawling cemetery, the memory of her drowning dream surfaced. Maybe it was a precognitive metaphor for how she felt right now: submerged, helpless, barely keeping her head above the oncoming torrential wave of chaos. But if it was also a sign, she could at least harness that knowledge to find her way out of this madness. *If I can't reframe this, I'll never make it through.*

She couldn't shake the sense that it was bigger than herself, that some unseen mastermind was orchestrating this bizarre phenomenon—a puppet master pulling unseen strings—and that her drowning nightmare the day before had been a warning.

Some research suggested that precognition came truly alive in the dream state, when consciousness was in flux and time non-linear, that there might be precognitive elements to every dream. Awake, it was much rarer to feel or see the future, although glimpses of it could signal through physical and mental hints: a humming pulse, a jittery gut, racing thoughts. Awake gut-level foresight, *presentiment,* was what Alice was feeling now: certainty in her every pore that something monumental was pulling her future forward.

Parking inside the garage, she fired off a text to Joe Sebastian, the man she'd been casually dating for a couple of years. For both, work typically overshadowed romance, but they understood each other; they felt relaxed enough to be themselves in each other's company:

Alice: *Need to get out of town.*

Joe: *What's going on? Just saw the have you dreamed of this woman? stuff.*

Alice: *No idea. I took 2 days off—to Greta's relief.*

Joe: *Come up here to Cassadaga.*

Alice: *Don't want to disrupt the bookstore biz.*

Joe: *Nah, slow day. I miss u.*

Alice: *Gotta pack my bags. See u soon!*

That was it. She threw a bag in the van and swung by her neighbor's place to pick up Luna, her black Lab, who'd been reluctantly lounging under someone else's watch. Usually, Alice found it hard to concentrate on a new semester with Luna around, but with her schedule now on hold for a few days, they could roam free and chill together.

Luna plopped herself onto the passenger seat, head lolling out the window, ears flapping in the breeze, blissful. Alice ran her fingers through the dog's fur as she navigated the streets, feeling strangely adrift now that work wasn't commandeering her every thought.

"Glad you're with me, girl. We're heading into the unknown."

Luna gave her fingers a quick, reassuring lick.

Alice let out a laugh. "Do dogs dream, girl?"

A quick bark was her only perfect answer.

Chapter 3

Cassadaga was unlike anywhere else in Florida—maybe even the world. It had been founded by a trance medium named George Colby, who claimed that the spirit of a Native American guide named Seneca, meaning "water beneath the rocks," had instructed him during a séance in Iowa to build a Spiritualist community in Florida. Braving the arduous trek from Iowa in 1875, Colby homesteaded a patch of West Volusia wilderness, and by 1894 had deeded 35 acres to what became the Southern Cassadaga Spiritualist Camp Meeting Association.

Today just one single road branched off I-4 and led straight into the enclave, with modest homes on either side whose yard signs read MEDIUM or PSYCHIC, ASTROLOGER or TAROT READER, each house its own little pocket of mysticism. The street sloped on into the heart of town, where a small rustic-looking bookstore stood on a corner, right across the street from the Cassadaga Hotel. The hotel spanned an entire block, short by big-city standards, but still impressive enough to command attention.

Built in the 1920s, Cassadaga Hotel was a relic from an earlier time when society's elite would flock here, desperate for messages from *the beyond*—seeking mediums' help to contact departed loved ones or unravel life's secrets about reincarnation and karma. Chicanery had been rampant in those days, but Alice had (so far) never sensed anything sketchy now.

Once she'd started half dating Joe, Alice had been introduced to several of the resident psychics through his mother who'd practiced here for three decades. Out of pure academic curiosity, she'd had readings with a couple of psychics, sampling different techniques and approaches. Some relied a little too heavily on cold reading techniques for her liking, and charged a little too much for their services, but they all seemed to genuinely want to comfort their clients.

Rolling past the hotel, Alice followed a shallow, curving hill toward Spirit Lake and the nearby park, perfect for letting Luna stretch her legs. Two other cars were parked by the lake: a man and a young boy fishing near the water's edge, and a woman casting a line some three hundred yards away. Alice pulled into a spot, let her dog out, and headed for the sidewalk that meandered through the trees.

Benches and signs decorated the path, offering snippets of Cassadaga's history and heralding its reputation as "the psychic capital of the world." Luna sniffed her way forward, nose solidly to the ground, until she caught sight of a squirrel and bolted after it in a blur of black fur. Alice loped after her, savoring the exercise. Around the next bend, she found Luna sitting upright patiently at the base of a tree while the squirrel chattered triumphantly overhead.

"He's laughing at you," Alice said. "Come on, girl, let's go to the bookstore. Joe's waiting."

Luna bounded into the backseat at the sound of Joe's name.

Alice pulled up the hill and parked at the side of Cassadaga Books. Luna leaped out before the engine had even died, bounded up the porch steps, and paused at the door, wagging her tail. The moment Alice opened it, Luna bolted past her, knocking her slightly in the process, then began scanning the aisles.

Alice spotted a stack of books under a sign that read *Banned Books*, wondering if any of the governor's minions might show up to spy on those who might dare to glance at one. Rumor had it they'd been dropping by some Orlando chain stores, issuing warnings—though the governor didn't dare outright fine the owners or press charges. Too risky for business.

"Luna! My favorite dog!" Joe's always calm voice carried from the back as Luna's yapping filled the air.

When Alice looked over, Luna was already standing on her hind legs, paws supported by Joe's arms, like they were dancing. Alice snapped a photo.

"I love this dog," Joe laughed.

"The feeling is obviously mutual."

Luna finally dropped her paws to the floor, then sat, gazing expectantly at Joe.

"Treat time," he reached into a jar on the counter for chicken-on-a-stick, one of her favorite treats. "You know the protocol, Luna."

Luna barked once, then gently took the treat from his hand. Joe scratched her behind the ears. "You're such a stellar dog. With a stellar human to guard you," he slid an arm around Alice's waist, pressing a light kiss to her lips.

In his early 40s, Joe Sebastian looked every bit like the life coach and bestselling author he was—tall, nimble, with green eyes and dark curls he pulled back into an unfussy ponytail. He and Alice had known each other since he'd taken one of her courses while working on his doctorate. After he'd snagged his Ph.D. in psychology with honors, they started dating. Sort of. The new academic credential gave him a certain level of clout with publishers, he told Alice, and indeed his books frequently landed on bestseller lists.

A door to the adjacent room swung open, and a woman with a curtain of poker-straight white hair and wide eyes stepped out. She propped a small sign in place that read *Tarot Lecture with Judy*. She spotted Luna, who'd moved in close, tail wagging.

"Oh my, you're a beauty!" the woman extended her hand.

"That's Luna," Joe said. "And this is Alice, her chosen human."

The woman turned to shake Alice's hand. "Pleasure to meet you. I'm Judy." Her eyes went wild and wide. "Holy shit. I dreamed about you."

Not again. Not here.

"What… what happened in the dream?"

"Brace yourself. It's a bizarre one."

"Name me a dream that isn't," Alice stated. "The more bizarre the deeper the meaning."

"You were showing me a six-card tarot spread I'd never seen before. I was sitting opposite you in a dimly lit room and your eyes were where your mouth should be, and they were different colors. I watched you lay out the cards, one by one, and when you laid each card down, their edges curled like they were alive. The characters in the cards twisted in agony and pleaded to be set free. You said they had always been free. They began to crawl out of the cards and move toward me with hungry eyes, but before they got to me—to eat me alive, I'm sure—mercifully, I woke up."

Tarot. Until this very moment, Alice had known little about it. "What was the spread?"

"Let me show you." Judy ushered her into the reading room. Spacious but intimate, it was set up with four tables, a neat row of pens and paper in front of 40 chairs. Snagging a deck, Judy fanned the cards face down on one of the tables. "Pick six."

Alice drew six cards at random. Judy arranged them into a pattern.

"I recall the spread in my dream, but don't recall precisely what you said or the specific cards you drew, only that you were laser-focused and precise. Let's see if this spread can deliver for you." She pointed to the first card, on the far left. "The Queen of Wands. You are a fire sign, perhaps, or have a lot of fire in your astrology chart? Wands represent fire."

"Yes, proud to come out as an Aries here, the baby, the first dream of the Zodiac. In both astrology and dreams, fire symbolizes energy, transformation, but also devastation and destruction. I'm assuming that is the psychological reference in tarot too?"

"You got it. Now, this card isn't literally you, but it does represent the current vibration in your life—how you're carrying yourself these days." Judy tapped a second card just below the first. "This will expose hidden potential or what you're beginning to manifest. With the Queen so close by, it suggests appreciation rather than realization, reaction rather than response. Not necessarily bad, just depends on context. Since you didn't ask a specific question, we'll consider this a general 'possible pathway' for your life."

Alice glanced down to see the Three of Cups. "And that means...?"

"Wands are fire, Cups are water-feelings, empathy, flow. In the Three of Cups, the dominant feeling is celebration and shared joy."

"People dreaming about me like I'm a sideshow. Doesn't feel so celebratory to me."

"Remember, it's *potential*," Judy responded. "The future isn't carved in stone. You get to choose. Think of it like this: if I picked up this tarot deck and dropped it, that's the deck's future, on the floor. But if at the last second, I change my mind and snatch it before it hits the ground, I've changed its destined outcome. Same principle with your choices."

Maybe that was how dream precognition worked, Alice thought: it showed you the most probable outcome, based on your current mindset, but always left room for a course correction if you made an intentional shift. It was a useful concept, and something that would slot perfectly into the first draft of her book.

"Everything going on around you," Judy tapped the card, "is telling you to trust your instincts. To answer the call from within. You must make an epic shift in how you see yourself. The person you once were—or still think you are—has already fallen away. You just need to acknowledge it. And that nudge will come through some kind of contract or meeting of like minds. Sorry I can't be more specific—but with any reading, it's *your* associations afterward that matter. That's rather like your dream interpretation stuff, isn't it? Personal associations before collective ones. The greatest dream dictionary is the one the dreamer composes themselves?"

Alice was already considering potential book titles.

Judy's finger drifted to the next card, and her brows rose. "This one's the Devil. To me, this represents desires, shadows, fears derailing you. It also warns of possible chaos from somebody whose intentions... Hold on. Let's see what your devil is up to. Pull another card."

Alice drew one more: the Tower. It looked like a metaphor for 9/11.

"Chaos," Judy said. "My clients always dread looking at this card more than Death or the Devil. But everything that happens, even disaster, can be used to your advantage. Either it's a lesson that strengthens you from within, or a blessing you didn't see coming. The Tower signals violent upheaval, yes. Maybe even destruction of relationships in the material sense— but not spiritual. It's the darkness before the dawn, the labor pains before the birth. Sometimes you need an explosion to blow apart whatever intolerable pressure has been strangling you. Boiling point. You must be lost before you find yourself." She paused. "Chaos is necessary for liberation and a new order to begin."

Chaos seemed like the perfect word for Alice's life now. She gestured to the next card on the table—the Four of Wands. "What about this one?"

Judy smiled. "What you scoop out. Beautiful. Even if everything feels shocking, chaotic, or disastrous right now, don't settle. It can still turn out great if you make the tough, independent choices instead of coasting along. You know how it goes: hard choices, easy life versus easy choices, hard life. If you can handle stepping outside your comfort zone, synchronicity will lead the way to astonishing progress and joy. But remember, it is only a *potential* future."

At least that sounded hopeful. Alice eyed the final card: the Nine of Cups.

"The wish card," Judy's voice was warm. "One of my personal favorites. Whatever you truly want, you can have, if you keep your perspective in check. The Tower, though, reminds that the path won't be simple. A period of uncertainty. Everything thrown up into the air to see how all the pieces land."

Joe frowned. "Is the Tower the worst card in the deck?"

"Every reader's got a 'red flag' card," Judy said. "The Tower is mine."

Great, Alice thought. "Those images are archetypal—I'm sure Jung would've approved. But thanks for the reading; it's been highly educational. And I'm sorry about showing up in your dream and taking over your tarot cards. I really don't know what's going on and why this dream stuff is happening to me."

Judy laid a hand on Alice's arm. "No apologies needed. I'm delighted with this spread and that it spoke to you. Thank *you* for being open-minded."

By the door, Luna basked in the delighted pats and coos as customers began to wander into the store. Once Judy had closed the doors for her presentation, Luna turned to Joe and Alice as if to say, *What now?*

"How about we grab a bite at the hotel dining room?" Joe asked. "We can eat out on the porch so Luna can tag along."

"Yes, if in doubt, eat," hummed Alice. "That's just what Willow always suggests in a crisis."

"That's a first. I've never been compared to my girlfriend's mother before."

"Who says I'm your girlfriend?"

"I'm the first person you called about this, right? Actions speak louder than words."

He was right; he often was. Research showed that highly intuitive personality traits often ran in families, and Joe was, after all, the son of one of Cassadaga's leading psychic mediums. "Okay. Let's say I am your girlfriend. Have you dreamt of me too?"

Joe looked decidedly uncomfortable.

"That's a lose-lose for me," he said at last. "If I say I haven't, you won't like it, and if I say I have, you will hate it."

Chapter 4

Joe Sebastian woke with a start, gasping, unable to forget his dream.

He'd dreamt of Alice before, but this time, the dream felt twisted, wrong. There was no joy, no connection, just an unsettling silence between them. In this nightmare, dream-Alice handed him something—a glowing object, so blindingly bright, he recoiled, dropping it.

It was a frog, grotesque, swollen and slimy. The symbol was obvious: rebirth, change. A creature that slithered from water to land, that started as a tadpole and grew into something else. Even in fairy tales, a frog could turn into a prince—but here, there was only horror, ugliness. The sensation of the frog was raw, almost tangible. Its skin was slick with heat, its weight a sickening pressure in his hand.

His dream-self whispered, *You.*

Before he could react, the frog leapt violently from his palm, crashing into his chest, its cold body scrambling up his throat, darting up to his head—then vanishing into darkness behind him.

Joe rubbed his face, the echo of the jump a lingering aftershock. The dream had been too vivid. Too *real*.

The frog had been a message, he was sure of it. But *what* it meant... the question burned. He sat up, the dream still alive deep inside him, like an itch he couldn't scratch. He stood, pacing his bedroom, but the more he thought about it, the more the dream seemed tied to something that had been unraveling in his life for weeks.

Alice.

The woman who had mentored him and who he was falling in love with was now playing the lead role in his dreams. She had challenged him, pushed him, left a mark on him. They had spent hours discussing the nature of consciousness, the human mind, and the possibility that there were truths lurking beneath the surface, truths that science had yet to grasp.

There had been something else during their debates, something unspoken, a spark, unfinished and simmering beneath their words. It went deeper than just the intellectual.

Her recent cryptic warning echoed in his mind. *Be careful, Joe. Some dreams are more dangerous than you realize.*

The words hadn't made much sense at the time. But in the aftermath of the dream, they resonated.

His phone buzzed. It was a text from Alice—the woman who never texted first.

Joe wasn't sure if he was intrigued or frightened. Whatever had begun in that dream was clearly not over. It was reaching out to him now.

She wanted to get out of town, fast. Before he could stop himself, he had invited her to come stay with him.

Just like that she was already on her way. The frog. Alice. The tension. Were they connected? Did Alice need him? Was his dream warning him?

He didn't care. He had to see her.

That evening as they waited for their meals on the hotel's porch, Joe recounted every detail of his hideous frog dream and how Alice's text that morning had come in while he was recalling it.

For the first time they had known each other, he saw a flicker of fear and uncertainty in Alice's eyes. "It's a warning—a key to something."

"Something unknown, possibly dangerous?"

"Yes. That frog is connected to something you and I both need to understand—before it's too late. It's not just a symbol. It's part of a bigger truth. And right now, we're both in its path."

Whatever Alice was talking about, it wasn't an intellectual exercise; it was real. It wasn't just about him, or her anymore.

Too many people were now dreaming, having nightmares, about her.

"I need your help," she whispered.

This wasn't what Joe had signed up for when he'd started studying with Alice, diving into the mysteries of the dreaming mind and over time falling in love with her.

But as she sat vulnerable before him, he knew it was his moment to step up.

"I need to get out of here," she urged. "I can't think straight. The academic and psychologist in me needs to make sense of all this—I need time and space, to feel in control again. Rise above. See the bigger picture."

"You are somewhere else."

"No, I mean out of Central Florida. To a place where people aren't dreaming about me and telling me about those nightmares. I'll dye my hair, change up my clothes and makeup, whatever it takes. I can't have everyone stopping and staring at me—because from what I've heard, everyone who's dreaming about me isn't seeing the same thing, and when they do see me, it's often nasty. Why?"

Joe spread his hands wide. "You're the Jungian expert."

"But you're the intuitive. What are you picking up?"

Joe opened Instagram on his phone. "Have you looked at it today?" He brought up the sketch that had started this whole frenzy. Except it wasn't Neal's drawing; she'd texted that one to him earlier. This version was similar, but also strikingly different.

"What I sense," he said, "is that someone or something is behind this. Like what Judy, the tarot card reader, said. Feels like some sort of contract—there's an agenda. But why is it all about you? You're not a threat to anyone."

"Where should I go?" pleaded Alice.

"St. Augustine." Joe reached for the first place that came to mind. "I can close the bookstore for a few days and go with you."

"I appreciate the offer, but you really don't have to tag along."

"Hey. I want to be with you, Alice." He covered her hand with his. "I don't want you going through this alone. Plus, let's be honest—I can already smell a potential book here. People know your dream face. This is the stuff of movies."

"Or maybe *my* first book, given I'm the one living the dream. Besides, I've always got Luna."

"Luna," Joe called, out glancing at the black Lab. "Can I come too?"

The dog barked once.

"I'm taking that as a yes," Joe moved closer to Alice. "We'll do a couple of days, stay in the old town, go through the fort. And if there is a book in all this, maybe we co-author. I've got the publishing connections; you've got the real-world experience. Together, we—"

He stopped midsentence, shutting his eyes.

"Joe? You, okay?"

Alice was leaning forward when Joe came to. "All good. Just sensed my grandmother's presence."

"What did your psychic antenna pick up this time?"

Joe sighed. "Again, let's clarify there's a difference between being *psychic* and being a *medium*. Psychics use their sixth sense to pick up on stuff most people can't see with their physical eyes. Mediums talk to, well... people who've crossed over. I happen to believe in the possibility of both."

"Tomato, to-*mah*-to," Alice waved a hand. "Belief is a powerful force. The mighty power of suggestion. Perception becomes reality. Hollywood calls it sixth sense, Christians call it prayer, scientists quantum physics, athletes call it will power, celebrities call it manifesting, and academics say intuition. No one denies it exists—or that it can energize someone enough to move mountains, solve problems, make great decisions, and achieve great heights."

"And what do you believe in, Alice?"

Alice closed her eyes, thinking. "I don't think I've asked myself that question enough. But right now, what immediately comes to mind are abstracts, like world peace, justice, compassion, equality, and, of course, on a personal note, the blinding theories of Jung. Anyway, you still haven't answered my question. I'm dying to know—what exactly did you sense? Because whatever you call your 'intuition,' seven times out of 10, it ends up being bang on, and I'd really like to understand why and how you can do that."

Joe cleared his throat. "She had a message, and it was a simple one. Flight rather than fight is the first step. I sense you need to get away from all this dream heat and do some research."

He shoved his half-eaten plate of food away. "Look, if what we've both picking up on here is real, getting away and becoming anonymous for a while is our best bet. You need to drive home now, disguise yourself and pack fast. Leave Luna with me. Time isn't on our side, because people are napping and sleeping all the time and every time they do..."

"I'm likely to make another unwanted appearance. You're right."

Joe walked Alice out to her car. Hugging Luna, she ducked behind the wheel and drove off.

"It's okay, girl," Joe crouched down as Alice's car merged with traffic and Luna pawed at the ground, whining. "She'll be back."

Whatever Alice was involved in, he was already too far gone to back out now.

On the road, Alice couldn't resist a quick search online. People were still dreaming about her; worse, there were signs it was happening further and further away, in other states. There were unconfirmed reports that even some powerful political figures had dreamt of her. What next, the Pope?

A viral rumor blowing up, dragging her into the crosshairs. In 2008, a sketch of a man whom thousands of people around the world had supposedly dreamed about for two years had gone viral before being exposed as a guerrilla marketing hoax. Was that what was happening to her?

And if so, who's behind it, and why?

Once she arrived at her familiar driveway, Alice felt some of her tension dissolve. In the kitchen, she grabbed Luna's dog food, moving around—but small details felt wrong: a dish out of place, a kitchen drawer not fully closed. She rushed to her bedroom. Nothing jumped out, yet everything felt *off*.

Maybe her rising anxiety leaving for work that morning had made her leave the house in this chaos.

She yanked clothes off hangers, scooped things from drawers, and crammed everything into a large bag, along with Luna's food. Going into her bathroom, she grabbed a pair of scissors, stopped, then cut off her long dark hair into an uneven bob.

She had done this haircutting scene once before in a dream. Déjà rêvé.

Grabbing purple and pink hair dye left over from a Halloween party, she rubbed it in, washing and blow-drying her hair. The result was not as pleasing as she'd hoped, but it was an effective disguise. She could always wear a cap, scarf, sunglasses. Shoving her laptop, blue lenses, and her Red Dream book into a bag, she took one last look at the life she was leaving behind.

On her way out, she noticed that the two front door locks looked strange. The top bolt—the security lock she never left undone—was unlatched. The lower lock, just the turn-button in the knob, wasn't fully engaged. She couldn't free herself from the feeling that someone had been here, an intruder in her home. If they'd tried to hide it, they hadn't done a good job.

Each passing second felt more ominous. Tapping open her security camera app, she rewound to early that morning. A few minutes after she'd left, the hazy video showed a man in a UPS shirt ringing the bell, rapping on the door, then glancing around and reaching into his pocket to withdraw a small gadget: some kind of electronic door opener. He aimed it at the locks. A quick flick, and he nudged the door open with his foot, stepping inside.

Cold fear crawled over her skin. Taking a screenshot, Alice texted it to Joe.

She sprinted to her car, heaved her heavy bags into the backseat, and tore out of the driveway.

Chapter 5

Alice wandered with Joe through the cobblestone streets of the Old Town. In the draining humid air of St. Augustine, they looked like normal tourists, dog in tow as they soaked in the quaint cafés, the town's charming history, the slow trickle of locals moving about their business.

But nothing was normal for Alice. Every time she saw her reflection in a shop window, she didn't recognize who was peering back.

The Airbnb they'd rented was a small, old building nestled between two tourist spots, tucked in an alley. Quiet. Dog-friendly. Most important, Joe had booked them in under a phony name. The odds of them being traced were slim, almost nonexistent, yet the possibility of someone recognizing her face from a dream was dangerously high.

Oblivious to their tension, Luna trotted beside them, distracted by the parade of new smells as they wandered aimlessly. Losing themselves in the anonymity of the crowd felt calming, at least for now.

At a small restaurant with a wide porch, Luna rested under the table, content to watch the world go by. But Alice pushed the same forkful around on her plate without really eating. Joe watched, helpless. Her shorter haircut and multicolored hair dye and blue lenses were an effective (if hilariously hideous) disguise, but only for those who didn't know her as well as he did.

"Talk to me, Alice," his voice cut through the restaurant's quiet hum of conversation. "You don't look like a cool professor anymore. That must feel strange. What's going on in your mind?"

When she looked up at him, her eyes were like deep pools. "I thought running was the answer. And so did you. But what if we are both wrong, and the answer is to stand up and fight back? When people say they dream about being chased, I always tell them to stop running, to turn around, and face their fear. To understand it, have compassion for it, because that's the only way to conquer it. But right now, I don't even know what my fear is. Or who's behind it. I don't know what to fight or even where to look."

"So, you're saying that's the task, right? To face the fear, understand it? To figure this freaky nightmare out?"

"You think I can figure *this* out?"

"I think you can figure anything out," Joe reassured. "But while you're busy wrestling with the intangible, we also need to look at the things we *can* touch. The things that are real."

He wasn't just talking about the dreams people were having; he was talking about the everyday reality they were running from.

No matter how much she wanted to hide, repress, deny, there were answers that could only be found if they stopped running, Alice realized. Whatever was chasing them was closing in on them fast.

"Let's kick things off with that video, the UPS guy your camera captured," Joe initiated. "I sent it to an FBI agent I've consulted for some of my books, for psychic detective case studies. He's going to see what he can dig up."

"You never fail to surprise me. An FBI agent, really?"

"He said we should stay clear of Orlando and Cassadaga. I didn't tell him where we are."

"Here's what I don't understand. When Neal dreamt of me, he and I were talking about the telekinetic episode that happened when Jung and Freud first met. In Judy, the tarot reader's dream, I was showing her a spread. You dreamed I gave you a shining object that turned out to be a frog." Alice tilted back in her chair. "I mean, I'm a Jungian expert, and I don't have a clue how anyone could manipulate specifics like that inside people's minds at night."

Nothing in Alice's training, nothing in the rational world, could explain any of this. Not the dreams. Not the symbols. Not the connections between them all.

"Study the image," Joe's soothing voice broke into her thoughts. "The secret is within it."

"You look like you're having an 'aha' moment."

"I am."

"Is your departed grandmother talking to you through your intuition again?"

"This time I'm not connecting to the other side, just using my common sense." He pushed his phone across the table, tapping the screen to pull up the sketch from Instagram.

"Study the image," he said again. "The secret is inside it. That's what my 'intuition' just told me."

They stared at the image: an abstract, disjointed sketch of a woman resembling Alice with unsettling eyes, her figure blending into something almost alive.

Alice closed her eyes. *Focus.* Words began to scroll behind her eyes, a message embedded in the image, hidden in plain sight. *I'm whatever you want me to be.*

She opened her eyes and repeated the phrase, as if it were a chant from somewhere far away. "I'm whatever you want me to be."

"What? I want to be terrified by a monster frog?" Joe shook his head. "C'mon, that makes no sense."

"The absurdity is what makes it so disturbing." The connection was there—*somewhere*—and she had to find it before it took her down with it.

A server placed bowls of soup and salad before them, and a small dish of water filled with ice cubes for Luna. The dog lapped at it greedily.

"Can she have a treat?"

"Sure," Alice smiled. Luna had a way of disarming everyone, her grounding, eager presence a breath of fresh air amid the chaos.

The server reached into her pocket and pulled out a large bone-shaped treat. Luna barked happily, sitting down with military precision and raising her right paw in a perfect salute.

"Wow, you're awesome," the woman kneeled to take Luna's paw, shaking.

"Thank you. That's what the paw means."

"Love it. Your meals will be out shortly."

The clues were coming thick and fast, but they were fragmented. Joe, even doing his intuitive best, was no closer to understanding what it all meant.

"I've been thinking about the dreams where you were drowning people," Joe remarked. "Water — emotions, the tides of feminine symbolism."

"This," Alice enthused, "is why you aced my courses. If this is subliminal, is the message somehow inscribed within the image itself, so people are primed when they see me in a dream to dream about their greatest fears?"

"That's my impression, yeah. But I don't have any idea how to prove it. Maybe my FBI contact will figure it out."

Joe refreshed the image on his phone. As the screen loaded, Alice saw his jaw tighten. She knew why: thousands more comments, just from Instagram. Given the reach of TikTok, Facebook, X, and all the others, each click, or share was like a ripple spreading out, reaching more people than they could fathom.

It wasn't just an image anymore; it was a curse. And they were at the center of it.

URGENT: Need your help with something, Joe texted his FBI contact. *Look at the attached image. She's my girlfriend. It's not gone totally viral yet but has been making rounds, and I think there's something malicious in it. Can you look and let me know what you find and who might be behind it?*

"You think the message in that image is *intended* for people to pick up?" Alice asked. "That whoever's behind this wants them to see it and then dream about me?"

"If it is, we're talking about a level of subliminal manipulation that goes far beyond anything I've seen. We're talking about something that messes with people's subconscious. Whoever is orchestrating this—whatever it is—has a hidden agenda. And it's not good."

Luna let out a small whine, her eyes flicking between them. Alice absently reached down to scratch behind her dog's ears.

"Do you think we're too deep in now?"

Joe just stared at the phone, willing it to ring. Time wasn't just running away from them, it was vanishing. With every passing second, the sinking feeling escalated.

It wasn't just a metaphor for Alice. The drowning had already begun.

After the meal, they wandered aimlessly once more through the narrow streets, letting the warm night air settle over them. Eventually, they found their way to a quiet park at the edge of town, where a serene lake stretched out like a mirror beneath the fading light. A dozen swans floated on the surface, their long necks swaying with the current, as if the world around them had ceased to exist. Joe bought a handful of duck pellets and tossed them into the water, watching as the swans glided toward the food.

Drawn to the water's edge, Luna pulled ahead, dropping onto her belly, her eyes fixed on the swans in silent invitation.

A swan with piercing eyes and feathers that gleamed white under the fading light swam up to Luna, then lowered its head and touched its beak to the ground just a few inches from her.

"Wow," Alice whispered. "Swans are dangerous. This is incredible. In dreams, they're symbolic of wisdom, of sensing the future, grace..."

"And love," Joe said. "Swans mate for life. And here comes the mate." Another swan glided toward them, reaching the shallows and waddling onto the sand with an almost regal elegance. It sat down beside Luna, who watched them with an intensity that suggested she understood something they didn't.

Alice raised her eyebrows at Joe. Wild swans were notoriously territorial—vicious, even—but here they were, behaving as though they were part of some strange, quiet ritual performed just for them.

The first swan—its mate now resting beside Luna—joined the second on the sand, settling beside the dog. Alice picked up another handful of duck pellets and approached the trio slowly, holding out her hand. Both swans looked at her, their eyes sharp but unblinking, before they returned their gaze to Luna. Neither swan moved.

"Luna," Alice murmoured softly, "tell them I won't hurt them."

Luna whined, inching closer to Alice from her spot between them. The swans shifted, moving even closer to her. Alice offered her hands again—one filled with the food, the other open, a gesture of trust. Slowly each swan swam closer and delicately took the pellets from her hand.

Luna barked happily, wriggling in excitement.

Alice threw the remaining pellets on the ground in a scatter, then stepped back to where Joe was standing. The swans lingered for a moment, feeding, then slowly slipped into the lake once more.

"That felt like a display," Joe whispered, "for you and me. A sign we're headed in the right direction. What do you think?"

Alice stared out at the water. "Mate for life?" There was a tension in her voice.

Joe's breath caught. "Uh… yeah."

Alice felt far away; she needed to feel the earth beneath her feet and return to the present moment.

"Alice? You alright?"

"People are waking up in the morning, and their first memory, thought and feeling is all about me. And those thoughts aren't positive—most of the dreams are slices of hell. I'm going to be honest, part of me feels *chosen*, like this is meant to happen. But another part of me feels violated. Everybody else sees my shadow before I see myself. Like with the swans... things can change in a heartbeat. I might be graceful and calm one moment, and then I could put you in danger. I could be deadly. It isn't safe to stick around with me."

"Life is never safe. And it's not meant to be. A ship is safe in harbor, but that's not what it was built for." Joe's eyes met hers. "Even when you've covered all bases, there are always unexpected bigger forces outside our control. All we can do is decide what to do with the time that's given us."

"Isn't that what Gandalf the wizard said to reassure a frightened hobbit?" Her shriek of laughter broke the tension. "I'm so glad I'm not the only one who has *Lord of the Rings* quotes on a loop in my head! Feels like my *unexpected adventure*."

"Soul mates," he said. "Elves and wizards at heart. And right now, even though you're saying, *you shall not pass*, my poor dreaming heart chooses to stay close to you."

They stood, watching the swans swim away to a distant horizon.

Life, love, dreams, danger—they were all intertwined in a way neither Alice nor Joe could explain. But wherever they were headed, for now at least, they would face it together.

The small dim Airbnb room felt like a prison as the hours dragged on that evening, Alice's phone constantly bleeping with alerts, messages, requests from people who were dreaming about her.

The clock on the wall ticked past midnight, the only other sound the faint hum of the air conditioner and clicking of keys. Joe sat at the small table, his eyes glued to his laptop, fingers flying. In her chair, Alice scrolled through social media feeds, searching countless threads and research papers to try to trace the origin of what she was tangled up in.

She couldn't escape the gnawing feeling that someone, somewhere, was watching them—her—and it was only a matter of time before they'd come for all the people she cared about. She glanced at Joe. "You sure we can trust the FBI guy you're working with? What if he's in on this? He could track you through your cell. Couldn't he?"

Joe's voice held steady. "I use a burner phone when I contact him. Like I said, I started doing that when I wrote my first true-crime psychic detective book. I'm a Method author." He glanced at her. "You'd be surprised how many law enforcement officers—and even governments—work with undercover psychics and remote viewers like me."

Alice turned back to her screen. The world was darker than it appeared, and no amount of caution seemed like it would be enough. But this was Joe's domain, his expertise. "Find anything?"

"Nope," Joe scanned his latest search results. "Nothing that ties it all together... yet."

Time seemed to freeze.

"Wait!" Joe cried out suddenly, his fingers flying across the keyboard. "This might be something interesting."

Alice went to him as he texted her a link. "Click on this."

Grabbing her phone, she tapped the link. The page loaded from an article on *If*, a popular online magazine known for its deep dives into science, culture, psychology, and speculative futures. It was about Carl Jung's theory of the collective unconscious, a concept Alice knew well. The idea that certain symbols, archetypes, and shared human experiences were passed down through generations, existing in a universal psychic space.

She scanned the article quickly, her mind racing. The author's name caught her eye—*P. R. Garcia*, currently at the University of Florida in Gainesville. A decade ago, Alice had asked Greta if they could invite the controversial psychiatrist to lecture to her students, a request Greta had immediately denied. He was bad news, Greta said; being associated with him was not a good idea if they wanted their department to stay well-funded.

Reading now, Alice felt she'd just stumbled upon something that was supposed to remain hidden, like the Holy Grail. The Florida University, bestselling dream author and Jung connection? What were the odds of this web of invisible threads linking him to her?

The article went on to explain Jung's belief that the collective unconscious was a vast, inherited reservoir of human experiences. The concepts of love, fear, life stages, death, and the archetypes that appeared in dreams—they were not just individual, isolated moments, but part of an eternal, shared human history. The longer Alice read, the more she felt like she was reading one of her own dissertations. The more light-bulb moments came.

It wasn't just the sketch. That image of her, the one that had been circulating on the internet, the one that was in her dreams, the one that had haunted her waking hours—it had become something more. It had become a toxic part of the collective unconscious. The very thing Jung had warned about. A psychic virus, a manifestation of the archetype of the stranger, a face that wasn't real, but was now being seen in the minds of so many people.

The image wasn't *exactly* Alice, but when people saw her in person, when they saw her online, when they dreamed of her— they saw *that* image. That sketch. A face that had somehow, insidiously, become *her* face in the minds of everyone who encountered it.

Everyone had dreams about strangers, of what is within them but not yet known and therefore feared. So now that sketch of me has become the archetypal image of a dangerous stranger, not just to the people who'd never met me, but potentially to everyone.

Landing on this article at this moment was no accident, Alice knew. Someone had *made* this happen. They were using Garcia's, and perhaps even her, research. Someone had deliberately or randomly turned her into an archetypal symbol, an idea, and now that idea had come alive.

It was almost like a modern version of *Frankenstein*, the first science fiction novel. Its author Mary Shelley had seen the story unfold first in a dream.

Joe was still scanning his screen, his face lit by the cold glow of the laptop.

She didn't know how she was going to defeat—not just understand, but beat this, but she would. They would.

There was no other choice. The future of everyone's dreams was potentially at stake.

Chapter 6

The scent of food jerked Joe from a restless sleep. His eyes snapped open, heart pounding, as the light flooding through the window told him it was probably around seven a.m. The bed beside him was cold and empty, but Luna was sitting at the foot of the mattress, staring at him intently, her tail thumping softly against the floor.

"Breakfast, right, girl?"

Luna barked once and trotted toward the door. Joe swung his legs out of bed, the sheets tangling around them. He'd had another dream of Alice. This time she was a grotesque serpent, her mismatched eyes glowing with an unnatural hunger. She had coiled around him, tightening her grip with every beat of his heart. As her mouth opened wide to reveal fangs, he realized—too late—that the woman he loved was not human but a predator, and he was her prey. He didn't have time to call forth more details of the nightmare. He could hear the clatter of pans from the kitchen.

When he emerged from the shower, Luna was waiting in the doorway, her head cocked as if asking what had taken him so long.

"Okay, I'm ready, Luna." She led the way into the kitchen.

Alice stood at the stove, flipping pancakes, the scent of eggs filling the air. The table was set, everything arranged with a care that seemed almost ritualistic.

"Espresso's coming up." Alice placed a bowl of food on the floor for Luna.

"What's the occasion?"

"I did some more research..." She gestured at her laptop on the desk by the window. "I think we need to drive to Gainesville today. University of Florida campus. Find out more about this Garcia guy. What do you know about him?"

"New York times bestseller knocked me off the top spot. Jungian psychology professor. Archetypes, anima and animus, synchronicity. Rumor is he was struck off?" He glanced at her. "An M.D. too?"

"Yep. Professor, just like me. But with one major difference," she placed the plate of pancakes onto the table. "He's a bestselling author. Three million and counting copies. The kind of success I could only dream about."

"That's what you've been doing since you got up at—what, 4 a.m.?"

"Three a.m. Luna needed to pee. Then I couldn't get back to sleep."

Joe watched her as she began buttering toast, quick and efficient. Her new hair color and style had subtly transformed her. She was trying to hide, or at least alter, her identity. It was working.

In the morning light, the hazy remnants of his nightmare echoing, he noticed something unsettling: she wasn't wearing her blue contacts. Her two-toned eyes—one brown, the other Mediterranean blue—were visible in all their strange intensity. That detail, that shivering mismatch, had made her image go viral. The world had fixated on her. But how did this Garcia guy know about it? How could he have known that private detail?

"What's your gut telling you about all this?" Alice asked. "What are you picking up?"

He closed his eyes, trying to tune in, to sense something that would give him answers. But his mind was filled with *nothing*—a hollow, oppressive silence.

"Joe? You okay?"

Okay, okay, okay—the word drummed like a warning. "I'm fine..."

Then a clear image came into his head: he saw himself and Alice, side by side, fists bumping at finding what they'd needed at the University of Florida campus. But the details were murky, like a dream half remembered. What had they found? Where?

He realized Alice was still waiting for an answer. "It feels like you are right and we should start our research immediately at the campus library." Luna barked once.

"Guess your dog agrees," Joe chuckled.

Alice drifted in and out of sleep as they drove toward the campus library, an eerie liminal dream scenario taking over her. She was a lost child, wandering through an endless shadowed library, her small hands pulling books off the shelves with reckless haste. *She needed to find them. Where were they?* She carried an armful of books to the nearest table. Setting them down, she glanced at the magazine rack, then grabbed the magazines she'd set aside and added them to her collection. The table stretched before her, cluttered with open books and magazines, their pages scattered like forgotten secrets. But the words were blurry. Unclear.

Alice paced around the table, flipping through magazines. Then the dream became lucid. She was conscious in her dream now; fully aware she was dreaming.

There it was: a specific article by Garcia in the science and psychology section, something about the collective unconscious. His name stood out, bold, like it was trying to reach her, but the text was hazy, slipping away just as she almost grasped the words. The harder she tried, the more she felt her lucid dream collapsing.

Then Alice was wide awake. She didn't know where she was until the lucid dream memory came back to her: the University of Florida campus. Two thousand acres. Over 900 buildings. Seven libraries. She didn't know which library had appeared in her dream, but she could go online and find out.

The seven libraries at UF house the largest academic resource system in the state. Specialized collections in science, health, art, history, and more. From agriculture to zoology...

Joe glanced over. "What are you doing?"

"I dreamed—a lucid dream—about a library," Alice explained. "I need to find it. There are seven libraries here. We should start with the science and psychology library."

"Map?"

"Got it." Alice pulled it up on her screen. "Take a left up ahead. Then a right, then two blocks. It's there."

As they drove, Joe reached over to massage the tension in her neck. "With all this lucid dream stuff, you're almost as psychic as I am."

She caught his hand and kissed the palm. "I don't think that's it. Like you, I just use my common sense and my dreaming mind helps me connect the dots between that and my intuition, and I have something invested in this. Whatever this is."

Parking was a nightmare. As they circled the lots, someone finally pulled out, but as Joe moved in, a white car cut in front of them, the woman inside it on her phone.

"No way," Alice screeched.

Joe jokingly put his finger on Alice's lips. "She's arguing with someone she cares about. Let her have it." He turned the wheel, moving on.

"I can't do that, Joe—I don't tune into people like you do. Maybe I lack the empathy gene," she protested. "Except when it comes to Luna. I'd much rather be with animals than people."

"Hey, *I* am a person," Joe urged, "and you are with me. Don't give up on your own species yet. And I didn't *know* she was arguing. It just felt like it, a calculated guess."

They found another spot and parked. Alice opened the back door, let Luna out and put on her service dog harness. "You're such a good girl, Luna."

Joe shot Alice a look. "She really understands you, doesn't she?"

"Maybe she's my soul dog."

Inside the science library, Luna stayed by Alice's side.

"What exactly are we looking for, Alice?" Joe queried.

"Anything by Garcia. Especially if it's not online." Instinctively Alice headed toward the science and psychology magazine section.

"We should start with their computer inventory for books," Joe said. "Magazines are a different story."

Alice nodded but listening to her gut subtly ignored his advice and walked over to the magazine shelves, scanning for anything that could be useful. Three rows of journals under "Psychiatry/Psychology." Most only went back 15 years. One swiftly caught her eye.

The May 2012 issue of *Psychiatric Journal* had an article by P.R Garcia titled *An Expanded View of Synchronicity*. The January issue of *Psychiatry for Pros* had his column, *The Big What If...*

Alice stroked Luna's fur. "Good girl. Settle here."

The dog's tail thumped against the chair as Alice flipped through the magazine.

There was the column.

The Big What If... by P.R. Garcia, M.D.

Imagine waking up to find your phone buzzing with messages, all saying the same thing: people are dreaming of a woman or a man who looks exactly like you. Strangers stop you, ask questions, demand answers. Who are you? What's going on?

In August 1942, long before cell phones, this happened to a Polish woman named Zofia. She was at a park with her children when others began staring. Finally, one woman approached, whispering: "I dreamed of you. You're a German agent..."

The woman's words tore through everyone present. Zofia froze. "I'm not.... I'm just like you. A Polish mother." But the stranger pointed at her, screaming, "She's one of them. We dreamed of her. She's a German agent."

The crowd descended on Zofia, tearing her apart. Her children fled. And in the aftermath, it was revealed: Zofia was part of a covert experiment to manipulate human consciousness.

Just as Alice was texting the article to Joe, he returned with a stack of books. "This guy is obsessed with Jung. You two really are a match made in heaven and hell, huh?"

Alice picked up a book with a torn cover from the pile Joe had dumped on the table: *The Story of Zofia*. "You ever hear of Zofia?"

"Nope. You?"

"No." Alice flipped through the first chapter. Garcia had traveled to Poland in 2011, seeking out Zofia's daughter Julia, who was then living in a nursing home. Julia had been there when the mob attacked her mother. She recalled everything— the terror, the screams, and the police who'd arrived too late to save poor Zofia.

Julia's sister Celina had died a few years ago. Celina's son Filip, a psychiatrist, had spent his career unraveling the mystery of the collective dream that had led to his grandmother's death.

Flipping through to the end, Alice read:

Filip believes someone close to Hitler's inner circle—well known for its fascination with the occult—had randomly targeted Zofia. By circulating photos of a woman with dark hair and unusual mismatched eyes—much like Zofia's—the traitor tapped into the collective angst of the Poles by running a series of experimental photos in an underground newspaper that identified Zofia as a secret agent. This person could have manipulated their collective consciousness, causing the dream that led to her death.

"Unusual eyes..."

Joe's voice was low. "Like yours. Freaky."

"It's not just strange. It's uncanny. A synchronicity, or something else."

"You ever want to visit Poland? Maybe a past-life memory?"

"I don't believe in past lives; not like you do." Alice shook her head. "I know you mean well, Joe, but let's deal with one dream at a time, okay?"

"I hear you."

Alice pointed at the book on the table. "This book—why is it out of print? Why isn't anyone talking about this? But it doesn't matter now. I think we're getting close to the beating heart of our mystery, the origin of it."

Alice suddenly felt breathless and in need of fresh air. "I'm starting to feel faint. Let's go. Luna needs a walk."

Joe nodded, "Food first."

Alice ordered Garcia's books online as they made their way out.

"For once I agree with your food first objective. Right now, food and a stiff drink sound divine," she said.

Chapter 7

During lunch at a quiet spot off campus, Joe typed out a quick text to a couple he knew from Gainesville. The Grangers: Aisling and Barnes. He thought of them as dream whisperers, though they were both licensed psychologists who had woven dream work into their practice. But there was something more about them — something otherworldly. They were exceptionally intuitive, psychic even.

You two free for a couple of hours? I'm in Gainesville.

Aisling responded almost immediately. *Barnes is with a client for another 30 minutes, but then we're free. What's up, Joe? Haven't heard from you in months.*

I took over the Cassadaga bookstore for Mom when her mother fell, broke her hip. She's looking after her now.

How's your grandmother?

Improving. Listen, I urgently need your and Barnes's insights on something.

A new book? Another true psychic crime you want to pick our brains about — or fiction this time? You know that's another way to mainstream the reality of the supernormal in our lives.

No. Something totally never seen before. Just finishing up lunch. See you within the hour.

Joe put the phone down, feeling more hopeful than he expected. He had to get things off his chest, and he trusted the Grangers would be able to help. They always had a way of seeing things others couldn't.

The waiter — a middle-aged man covered in tattoos of snakes that spiraled across his muscular arms, his neck decorated with Zodiac symbols — approached the table. He took their orders from the basic Mexican menu.

"And water for the dog," Alice said.

"Got it." He dug into his pocket, producing a couple of dog treats.

Luna perked up, tail swishing in excitement, then gently took the treat. She sat back down on her haunches, watching as Alice set the second one on the table.

"Cool name. Luna. Is she a Cancer?" the waiter asked.

Alice shook her head. "Not sure when exactly she was born. I just liked the name. It means Moon. Of course, cancer is ruled by the moon."

"I'll bring her some iced water," the waiter said, disappearing into the kitchen.

Never judge a book by its cover, Alice reminded herself. Her first impression of the waiter had hardly been that of an astrologer or a gentle animal lover.

Joe turned to Alice. "I'd like you to meet a couple of friends just outside of town. Barnes and Aisling Granger. Psychologists. Dream experts. They might be able to help us with all this."

"How do you know them?"

"They started as clients of my mom's. Then one day they came to Cassadaga when she was on vacation, and I was working the store. They became my clients after that."

"Your clients?"

Joe's eyes held something unspoken. "At first, they wanted to study me. Then they decided they wanted to learn from me. It's... we've been kindred spirits ever since."

Alice tried to be casual. "Have they dreamed about me, too?"

"No idea." He wiped his mouth with a napkin. "Guess, we'll find out."

"Well, it can't hurt to brainstorm. If you trust them, let's go see what they have to say about all this."

The waiter returned, Luna's water bowl clinking softly in his hands.

Alice's mind was already tangled up in questions. Whatever insight Aisling and Barnes had to offer, the chances were high that it wasn't going to be easy or simple. Nothing about this situation was.

The Grangers' house sat in the middle of an aging neighborhood just outside Gainesville, where cobblestone roads wound between towering live oaks that Alice found herself wanting to embrace. The scene was dense with the scent of earth, roses and old leaves. In the backseat, Luna hung her head out the window, her nose twitching in the breeze, tail wagging with joy.

At last Joe pulled into a short driveway, parking behind a pair of identical VW Tiguan vans, one fire-engine red, the other a dark, brooding blue.

The A-frame house loomed before them, the windows so large they seemed to swallow the sunlight. As soon as Alice opened the door, Luna bolted, ears flat, nose on overdrive. Heading straight for the nearest window, she caught sight of something inside and barked once, then twice.

The door swung open.

A slender middle-aged woman with shoulder length auburn hair and brilliant sea blue and green eyes stood there, arms wide. "My God, you look like Nika."

Luna yelped, a streak of black fur shooting into the woman's arms. The woman sank to her knees, hugging Luna to her chest, smothering her face in sloppy kisses. Alice had never seen Luna react this way to anyone. The woman cupped her face, gaze locked onto the dog's eyes. "Are you Nika?"

"Who's Nika?" Alice's voice felt distant to her own ears.

The woman rose, smiling brightly, and held out a hand. "I'm Aisling. You must be Joe's surprise."

"Alice. Alice Sinclair." Alice shook her hand.

Aisling stepped back; gaze fixed on Alice. "Wow. Great disguise, but I can see right through it. You're that stranger everyone's dreaming about. I dreamed of you too. In my dream, we were flying without wings in space together. The higher we soared, the larger you became, and the smaller I shrank. I was scared I might disappear altogether, but then you told me to stay calm. You said I would see Nika, my beloved dog, who I had to put down years ago, really soon."

"How many years ago did she pass. I'm so sorry about that?"

Aisling's voice was quiet. "Four years. Six months, three days."

Alice stared. "I adopted Luna four years ago from a rescue organization in South Florida. She was just a puppy, rescued from a kill shelter. I'm not sure about reincarnation—so many dogs and cats out there born unwanted, needing a good home—but that's an astonishing coincidence. I'm glad she found me."

Luna had settled between them, watching them both as they spoke. Sinking to the ground, she rested her head on her front legs, until her head shot up: Barnes Granger, an impressively tall man with penetrating dark eyes and an impatient air about him, had appeared, a black cat trailing behind him.

"That's Nala," Barnes said of the cat.

Luna sank down again.

The cat strolled right up and sniffed her, gave the dog a commanding glance, then stalked away.

"Maybe that's past life too," Aisling chirped.

The four of them gathered on the back porch. Aisling poured them each a cup of strong coffee, giving treats to Luna and Nala. Even the animals seemed to be pensive, as if they knew something was about to unfold.

Barnes spoke first, "I dreamed of you too, Alice."

"What was the context of the dream?" Joe asked.

"Was I drowning you?" Alice couldn't help herself from asking.

Barnes shook his head, but something in his smile made Alice uncertain. His graying beard and lean frame were those of a man in his mid-fifties, but his body was that of someone far younger. "Stranger than that. I was wandering through a dense and dark forest. I found a treasure chest, overflowing with jewels and banknotes, but something felt wrong—too wrong to touch.

"I turned away, and there you were, standing still, your hollow blue and brown eyes staring right into me, trapping me with their energy. You told me that you were a cursed nightmare in the collective unconscious, and that there was no escape from you.

"I tried to run away, toward a mountain in the distance, but the ground shifted beneath my feet, pulling me under, until I was buried alive. I could only see a tiny window of light, but I wasn't going to give up on that light.

"When I woke up, I was still gasping for breath. Aisling was as terrified as I was—she told me that I had sat up in my sleep and turned to look at her, my eyes were wide open, and I had this menacing grin. She freaked out. She tried to wake me, but she couldn't."

"The forest in dreams is never random." Alice's mind was turning over the symbols. "It represents a journey into the unknown, a place where you're searching for something you can't quite grasp. It's a symbol of confusion, or perhaps a fear of losing your way. And the treasure? That's secret knowledge. Your unconscious mind is offering you a glimpse of something vital, something life changing." Her voice grew softer. "And the mountain? It's a challenge. A symbol of something you must overcome, a final obstacle before you reach clarity. Buried alive. A metaphor for feeling weighed down by responsibility."

"You're quite the symbol analyst," Barnes responded. "But did listening to my nightmare shed some light, ignite any emotional response within you?"

Alice felt only blank. "I don't think so."

Barnes sighed. "That's a pity. You see, despite the harrowing ordeal when I was in it, the key thing for me and what kept me going, was that I never lost hope. That was the feeling I got.

The speck of light was still there at the end of the tunnel in my dream, even if it seemed like it was fading fast. And from everything I know about dreams, it's the emotions they provoke that matter most."

Alice nodded slowly. "Joe says you two are experts in dream analysis. Are you Jungian?"

Aisling's eyes glinted. "Yes, but we're not limited to Jung. There's a whole world of dream analysis before and beyond him, Alice."

"I know of other schools," Alice argued, "but for me, Jung encompasses them all. His vision was vast."

Aisling's smile didn't falter. "Doesn't surprise me. You're entrenched in academia and Jung's the one—along with Freud—academia has welcomed, rejecting other equally profound voices. We've had our disagreements with the establishment but have learned to compromise and work with it." She shrugged. "Most of what's being discovered about consciousness and dreams is buried in jargon. We've made it our mission to break it down for anyone who wants to understand."

Alice ran her fingers through her hair, glancing at Luna. The dog had settled right beside Nala, still watching them intensely. "Well, at least you two had more positive dreams about me. I mean, flying in space and the hope of hidden treasure. I'll take that over blood sucking vampires and serial killers."

"We're steeped in dream analysis," Barnes clarified. "We've never feared exploring the bold frontiers of the unconscious, the unpredictability of the dreaming mind. But we are in the minority. I don't want anyone to get complacent about the dangerous potential surfacing here. All our clients have reported nightmares about you. That's why we need to stop whatever this is, because nightmares have a habit of making the most rational person think or act in an irrational way. Only this morning, one of my long-term clients, a sensible stoic guy struggling with his sexuality, sent me this alarming text. Barnes reached for his phone, scrolled, then read out the message:

Dr Barnes, something incomprehensible surfaced from the dark corner of my mind last night. You always encourage me to share my dreams with you, and I am eager to discuss it. I felt the weight of what I believe to be a succubus, her mismatched eyes burning with this unearthly hunger as she crept toward me. Her breath felt cold. Her fingers slid over my chest. It was suffocating. Her voice was like a melodic whisper, and she promised pleasure and doom in the same breath. She kissed me—but her kiss stole more than my breath; it took my soul. And even worse, when I woke up, the sensation was still lingering, the terror still clawing at me. I couldn't help wondering if it had really been a dream or if something darker had reached into my being and I need to contact a priest for an exorcism. Or should I seek out an expert in alien abduction? I'm scared. I can't forget this foul dream. Please advise.

Alice sighed. "Clearly, I have now become the monstrous feminine. The succubus. The alien. In times past, I would have interpreted these kinds of dreams as unexplored aspects of the dreamer's personality struggling to be recognized, or a feeling of being the odd one out and having to give up your identity to fit in. The weight of your persona literally crushing your soul. But now these pop psychology explanations feel like they don't come close to touching what is unraveling here."

The others seemed to sense what Alice was about to say next.

"Joe mentioned you might just have a theory about why I'm the woman lots of people are dreaming about."

Aisling exchanged a glance with Barnes, then nodded. Alice felt the connection between them, electric and unspoken.

Barnes's voice was like a stone dropped into a still pond. "My gut response is that it's not just one collective unconscious anymore. I believe the collective has ripped into two and there are two forces at play now, and for some reason you Alice are caught in the middle of them. One that embraces individuality and freedom, and one that thrives on power and control and taps into or feeds on the energy of people's anger and pain. The second group is getting louder, more aggressive, and more afraid of anyone who doesn't share their perspective—and after all, perspective is reality. Women especially are becoming targets. Forced into the 'traditional wives' box by those who want to push women back to the '50s. *The Handmaid's Tale:* that's their vision of the world."

"But Jung never spoke of a divided collective," Alice said. "Not even in the darkest days of WWII. Not when the world was closer than it has ever been before or since to cleaving in two."

Barnes agreed. "Fear of the 'other' or the 'stranger' seeped from sporadically to permanently into the collective unconscious back then like a seed in the soil. But now it's grown from seed to shoot. It has taken its first breath and been given oxygen to breed by social media. It's now a full-scale battle for validation. For control. Outside in versus inside out. Validation for externals versus inner empowerment."

Aisling concurred, "The noise of this materialistic, divisive, truth averse society is drowning out everything else. We— intuitive academics, psychologists, psychics, empaths, introverts and highly sensitive people like you, Alice and Joe with open minds and hearts—are being driven into the shadows. We used to be the shamans. Now we're the outcasts."

Alice nodded and closed her eyes.

"I first came across Jung when a friend handed me a book about *I Ching*," Aisling continued, "the Wilhelm edition. Jung wrote the introduction, and in doing so brought to the West the concept of synchronicity. I read it in one day, and something in me clicked, a lightbulb moment. It explained so many inexplicable moments in my life. After that, I became obsessed. I devoured it all, started writing and talking about it. I couldn't stop thinking about the transformative potential of synchronicity and the secret power of nocturnal dreams. So, I completely understand where you currently are with your research, but you will in time when you are ready to move on see the limitations and seek other perspectives. Alice, you're like Zofia — the Polish mother who..."

"We know about her," Alice fired back. "I don't want to end up the way she did."

Joe, sensing an undercurrent of tension between Alice and Aisling seized the opportunity to break into their conversation, "We just came from the UF campus. We found the story there about her. But what doesn't add up is how the person or organization behind the image of Alice could've created something so *specific*."

Without a word, Alice removed her contacts, then raised her eyes — unfiltered, exposed. "And the creator of this whole thing somehow got the color of my eyes *exactly* right. I've worn contacts since I was 14 to hide them. To blend in, be normal. To look like everyone else. I'm embarrassed by my eyes. I've learned the hard way that *difference* — it can't co-exist in peace." Her voice cracked. "I hide them because I'm a living reminder of how terrifying and isolating difference can be."

"Your eyes," Aisling's voice was a whisper, "they're breathtakingly beautiful, Alice. They're what make you *unique* — the windows to your soul. Why hide them?"

"Because my mother thought it was best if I didn't stand out. And she was right. People stare. They get scared — like I'm cursed or something. You know that famous Coleridge dream inspired poem, *Kubla Khan*, where he writes, 'Close your eyes in holy dread, weave a circle round him/her thrice'? Coleridge might as well have been describing *me*."

"Have you ever thought," Aisling declared, "that your belief that you don't fit in, or that your eyes will terrify others, is exactly why all of this is happening to you? What you unconsciously believe about yourself — you attract it. Manifestation 101."

"I'm a psychology professor, I know self-talk and buried bias have great power and show up in weird dreams. Maybe, when this is over, I'll get some more counseling—but right now, Aisling, I haven't got time for navel gazing therapy. I have a much bigger problem to solve first."

"There's nothing bigger than how you see yourself," Aisling replied softly. "But you're right. We need to get practical now. This isn't some dream. It's happening in the real world. It is a living nightmare. A nightmare in danger of coming to life, if Barnes's uncharacteristic sleepwalking episode is anything to go by. One reason intuitive people are often sidelined is they keep their heads in the clouds, forgetting that their feet are still on the ground—and that's where the action, the progress, the future is forged. We are what we do, not what we think or feel or even what we dream. So, what are we going to *do* about this living nightmare? Are we going to sit here and discuss it forever, or are we going to act this time? Escape woo-woo land. Walk our talk at last?"

The room fell silent, watching as Alice quietly re-inserted her blue lenses.

"We need to confirm who's behind this," Joe pressed. "That's the first step. And Alice... I must ask—could the person who created this image somehow be connected to you? Know about your unusual eyes? Any past lovers or childhood or family friends or colleagues or even your doctor or optician? I mean, you have never introduced me to your parents. I once heard you speak to your mom on the phone, but you haven't seen her in months. And you have never mentioned your father, so I always assumed you were raised in a single parent family. Were you adopted? We never really did our past-lives conversation."

"Not adopted, but abandoned before birth," Alice stated. "My mom was 22, recently graduated, and pregnant. The guy took off, never looked back. Never wanted to know. She raised me alone. Around the same time my grandmother also found out her husband—my grandfather—was leading a secret life, had another wife and kid somewhere. To show solidarity and to protect me from the reaches of my grandfather and father, she ditched her birth name, Willow Dodd, and took her mother's maiden name, Sinclair."

"What else do you know about your father?"

"Zero. Nothing. Nada."

Aisling implored, "Not even a name?"

"Nope. My mom never spoke of him. He was a ghost. The one time I really asked or pushed to know more about him, I think I was 12 or 13 at the time, she broke down. So, I dropped it. I couldn't bear to see her upset. Then, as the years rolled by, it stopped mattering. He just wasn't important. I stopped hoping for him or thinking about him at all. Not until now."

"You think this could be intentional?" Joe asked.

Barnes shook his head. "Not intentional. But I think it might just be some kind of synchronicity again. Like the universe is saying to you: *You don't know your dad? Let me take care of that for you.* Or: *He doesn't know his daughter. Let's fix that.* Did your mom ever send him a picture of you? Maybe a baby photo, something that would have shown your eyes? Maybe that detail stuck with him, unconsciously."

"I'll text her," Alice was already pulling out her phone.

"Shouldn't you at least call her for something this serious?" Aisling exclaimed, "or better still, do the human thing and meet her in person?"

"She's in the U.K. right now. I can't exactly call her and her internet connection is likely to be shaky. Text is all I've got. We really haven't got time to be super sensitive. I lived in Britain until I went to college, and we moved back to the U.S. She's in the U.K. now, just visiting old friends she sees once or twice a year."

"Garcia is British born," Joe mused.

"Garcia?" Barnes was suspicious. "You mean that rogue psychiatrist who dominates the book charts and talk shows when it comes to dreams?"

Was my dad's name P Garcia? Alice texted.

The answer came immediately:

Pedro Garcia.

"Good God. My mom just told me his name is Pedro Garcia."

Why are you asking me THIS now? Time and place, love. Time and place. WTF?

Cause he may be the one who created the viral image of the woman with odd eyes —me—that everyone's dreaming about over here. Did you ever send him a picture of me as a baby? One where he could see my eyes are different?

Nope. He made it clear he didn't want to know anything at all after I got pregnant. Wanted me to have an abortion but I couldn't. I chose you over him. Best decision ever.

Did you have any contact with him after that?

No. Nothing.

How come you never told me his name, Mom?

A minute passed, but Alice could see her mother was typing and pausing, typing and pausing.

Believe it or not, I did love him, and he broke my heart. It hurt too much to talk about him. I had to stay strong for you.

We shouldn't be texting about this. Come to the UK. Get away from the dream madness. Let's talk face to face.

I'll see. Love you, Mom.

I love you too. On the tube and will lose signal soon, but before I go, a tidbit he's obsessed with Jung, like you. I think he moved to Florida a few years ago. I often wondered and worried if you would find each other. Hotshot author these days. Guessing you know all that, though.

Alice read the text out loud to the group. "My father... *Pedro Garcia*... a Jungian psychologist... and he's in Florida right now. What are the odds?"

"Fascinating," Aisling interjected. "So maybe this viral image—a woman with one brown eye, one blue—could be his unconscious way of trying to find the child he never knew. Alice... are you okay? You're looking a little pale."

Joe helped Alice to a chair. "Can't know for sure but so far this makes as much sense as anything else we've come up with. Barnes, could you give Alice a glass of water?"

"I keep thinking about Jung's scarab story," Barnes mused, handing Alice the glass.

Amira had told her the story days ago, but it felt like a lifetime. "So, is this my scarab moment?"

"Could be," Barnes exhorted. "But the only way to know for sure is a DNA test. The eyes don't lie. Even then, this Garcia guy may still have absolutely nothing to do with the image. He could be as innocent as you and caught up in something he doesn't understand."

Alice had the name of the man who might—*might*—be her father—and even the creator of all this chaos. A psychologist. Living in Florida. Jung his specialty. Could it all be connected?

The doorbell rang. Aisling stood up instantly. "I'll get it. I'll get rid of whoever it is."

Luna suddenly growled, then sprang to her feet behind Aisling. Aisling opened the door to a stockily built imposing man waving a badge.

Alice craned to hear what he was saying.

They were looking for Alice Sinclair to discuss a case, the man was saying. A man had been arrested for murdering his wife. He had confessed but was pleading not guilty. His lawyers were claiming that he had not been in control of his actions, because in a series of recurring nightmares, Alice had repeatedly told him to kill his wife. He had sought medical advice and been put on a course of sleeping tablets, but they had just made his dreams of Alice—the woman with evil mismatched eyes—more extreme. They were calling it 'A dream made me do it' defence.

Everything went black.

Alice found herself in her lecture hall with rows and rows of attentive students. Suddenly the doors burst open. A giant version of herself, with pink and purple hair and mismatched eyes, entered the lecture hall. Hollow eyes locked on Alice; she couldn't move. The students started screaming and scattering, but the vision of Alice seemed to feed on their pain and panic; it just grew stronger, taller. Alice crouched down to make herself as small as she could; she scanned for a desk to hide under, but the dreaded vision of herself was now right in her face. "You can run, but you can't hide me," it roared, its voice distorted. Alice opened her mouth to scream, but no sound came out. Then she noticed her left hand was melting...

When Alice opened her eyes, she was lying on the floor. Luna was licking her left hand. Joe was cradling her head. She was prone to anxiety blackouts he was telling Aisling and Barnes as they crouched beside her; they needed to keep the stress to a minimum.

Behind them Alice saw the looming presence of the man with the badge. His strange brown eyes met hers.

They were not strangers. They had met before.

Chapter 8

Pedro Garcia sat in a quiet corner of a downtown Orlando café. Controlled and elegant at nearly sixty, he had strikingly handsome features, pale blue eyes, dark hair with just enough gray to be distinguished, a shadow of designer stubble. The sharp cut of his Armani suit complemented it all perfectly. Something cold and effortless about him evoked indolence and authority, as if he were a character straight from *The Godfather*.

He sat scrolling through his phone, detached, waiting for his contact to arrive. The woman's face he'd created had infiltrated the dreams of Floridians far beyond anything he'd anticipated, and it was now being linked to a woman called Alice Sinclair. It had been only 72 hours since he'd dropped the Instagram post, and even though he had simply created a generic sketch of a youngish woman, with his unique subliminal messaging signature encoded within it, already thousands were claiming they'd dreamed about her. He'd added a crucial twist: those different colored eyes, a rare condition but one that would immediately find a likely target.

As a psychiatrist, Pedro felt this was the perfect illustration of how easily the unconscious — untouched by logic or reason — could be manipulated. And how effortlessly the group mind swarmed to the same conclusion.

And the most direct route for that group manipulation? Nocturnal dreams, of course. To Pedro, it seemed almost laughably obvious. He couldn't believe no one else had not gone big on this idea before, with real money and real power backing it. But then, logic and reason had no place in the dream realm. Everything there boiled down to emotion, intuition, and creativity — imagination.

Forget all the waking-world rationality. Even if you never recalled a single dream, your mind was still going to have several every night. So, if you discovered a way to infiltrate dreams, you could set up camp right inside someone's subconscious without their being aware of it. And once something lodged itself in the subconscious—regardless of the conscious mind's denial—it became what the psyche inevitably sought out, what it needed to know itself better. Or at the very least what it accepted as normal.

And if enough people invited it into their subconscious, over time it became an archetype, a part of the collective or shared unconscious.

Night visions offered the dreamer a snapshot of their subconscious mindset—a potent magnet for change. The best part? Apart from a handful of niche experts, especially Jungian types like himself, the mainstream consensus had always dismissed dream decoding as nonsense, chalking it up to random firings of the brain or "woo-woo." Given this natural cover for dream manipulation, Pedro wasn't the least bit shocked when a wealthy mystery benefactor had finally caught on, got fired up by his research and hired him to take it to its logical conclusion and run this localized experiment. The benefactor was now eager to find out how and why dream hacking worked—and more importantly, what Pedro could deliver on next.

If you could manipulate dreams, you could potentially manipulate minds. That simple truth had them all eating in the palm of his hand. Without a doubt, for the right price—well above the 50K in cash he'd already pocketed—Pedro would work on something infinitely bigger now, and perhaps even reveal his unique method to them.

It looked like things were heading in the right direction. His first pitch had worked. Florida was alive with dreams of this Alice woman. Pedro's credentials now spoke for themselves. If anyone could hack into people's dreams, he was the one.

It was hilarious—ironic—because for years now he himself could barely remember his own dreams. Sometimes he missed waking up with them on his mind, as he had done when he was young.

As a child, he'd loved bedtime, because sleep meant dreams— and dreams were magic. They gave him an opportunity to dream himself away from poverty and hardship.

But it had been years since he could remember his dreams. He brushed off the feeling that he was missing out on something valuable—dreaming was for the gullible.

Pedro had been born to Cuban parents who emigrated to the U.K. He'd grown up with a crisp British accent, then married an American and spent the last few decades Stateside. His wife was not just any American—a former Miss Florida.

His fascination for researching the dreaming mind and the power of suggestion had carried him through university. There he'd ended up proposing a radical theory, something science still hadn't been able to nail down: that the reason we sleep isn't to rest, per se, but *to dream*.

Pedro was one of the first psychiatrists to fully back the notion, with a few unfunded but credible peer-reviewed studies, that the dreaming mind acted not only as an internal therapist but also as a kind of brainstorming powerhouse, forging insights that simply couldn't happen in the waking state. So, when a person rolled out of bed in the morning with a new solution to the problem they'd been wrestling with, it wasn't because they'd slept on it, but because they'd *dreamed on it*.

Hell, even Einstein himself had said the initial inspiration behind his theory of relativity had been a dream of cows bouncing on an electric fence in wave formation. Awake, people often missed the subtle connections crucial to problem-solving, because the conscious mind blocked anything that defied logic. In the dream state, though, those same ideas slipped through the cracks, reappearing in the form of symbols. And symbols, like the emotions powering them, blew logic out of the water. They demanded an intuitive and imaginative approach, not a rational one. A leap of faith.

Pedro's theory of "dream power" spoke to the mainstream — catapulting him, for the first (but not last) time, to the top of the *New York Times* bestseller list with his debut, *Dreams Alive*. His follow-up, *The Big Dream Game*, also soared in sales. Of course it did. Everybody dreams and everybody has had that dream they want to know the meaning of.

Yet the same commercial success that had put him on daytime talk shows and bookstore tours only deepened his rift with his academic peers. Their book reviews were brutal, dismissive, one after another accusing him of "dumbing down" and misrepresenting sleep and dream research. He was a pseudo-scientist, a sellout, they said, lumping him with other woo-woo people like alleged psychic medium and fellow *New York Times* bestselling author Joe Sebastian. Some critics in the psychological association even called for Pedro to lose his license, as if publishing a layman-friendly dream-decoding book were a crime.

The academic rejection stung more than he would admit. He kept his Florida university post but always felt that he was walking on eggshells with the university board.

At first, his intentions had been pure. Pedro genuinely wanted the world to fall in love with the secret power of dreams — their own private portal to the unconscious mind, both the collective and the personal one, and thus true self-understanding. Self-knowledge, after all, was the root of all wisdom. He had also hoped to pioneer self-help techniques for mainstreaming the "holy grail" of dreamwork: knowing you're dreaming while you are in a dream.

Pedro had effortlessly mastered lucid dreaming in his early 20s during a six-month retreat at a Buddhist monastery, where monks had taught him the art of meditation and yoga Nidra conscious-sleeping techniques. The monks mentored him on ways to dreamscape—actively shape the content of his dreams—in turn shaping his own unconscious and what it was attracting. He emerged electrified, driven by a grand vision to change the world from the inside out. If children learned these techniques from an early age, he figured, because of their natural inclination to find it much easier to suspend disbelief, people could reclaim inner power on a massive scale. There would be far fewer cases of depression. He could see the possibility of teaching dreamwork in prisons, helping inmates confront their "shadow" side, to recognize but not identify with it, and thus end up making better life choices and lowering crime rates.

Pedro championed the power of dream journaling and the power of rescripting one's anxiety dreams in their waking state, reminding anyone who'd listen that daydreaming or mind-wandering was just more conscious dreaming, a way to create unconscious shifts. The brain couldn't tell the difference between sleeping and waking, Pedro loved to say. So, if a person woke up tangled in an anxiety dream, there was no need to panic—the dream wasn't literal or precognitive. It wasn't some prophecy; it was simply the mind conjuring up a scenario likely to happen if that mindset continued—because what a person unconsciously believed was what they tended to manifest. All they had to do to change this was to rewrite the dream's ending while they were awake, effectively rewiring their own unconscious.

The human brain always followed where your unconscious belief led it. Simple as that.

But it became abundantly clear that his peers would never rally behind Pedro's grand, utopian vision, never embrace him as the next Jung or give his theories the respect they deserved. So, Pedro's passion for ushering in an enlightened dreams-alive world gradually withered into distant memory.

He didn't stop writing about dream power, of course; it was his meal ticket. He got to travel the world, signing bestsellers for lines of adoring fans. But the academic rejection had soured his love for dreams; even recalling them stung, like salt in an open wound.

Pedro stopped writing them down on waking, stopped trying to remember them, stopped himself from analyzing them the rare moments some still broke through. Eventually, he woke up every morning with no dreams on his mind. Nothing but a desire for power, status—and money.

Just as Pedro tired of seeing Alice's face on his phone, his Cuban espresso arrived, accompanied by a serving of snacks only a true Cuban café would serve—small piping hot empanadas, neat slices of *medianoches*, and a handful of malanga chips.

Minutes later, Ward Newman sauntered through the door.

He looked like a stereotypical sun kissed blonde, brown eyed, Central Florida businessman: pack slung over one shoulder, no jacket, khakis and a button-down blue shirt, an oddly patterned tie, and sunglasses resting atop his head. Spotting Pedro, he slipped his phone in his pocket and hurried over.

"Hey, Garcia."

"Hey yourself."

Dumping his backpack on the floor beside the chair, Newman sat down. After the server had taken his order, he leaned toward Pedro. "Over one hundred thousand reports in just 12 hours. We're seriously impressed. Keep this under wraps, but word is even the Senator of California has been dreaming about the woman. Top secret."

"The Senator, huh? Bloody hell. *I'm* impressed with myself." What started in Florida clearly wasn't staying in Florida. "I was just testing the waters, showing you what I can do. But we should pull the plug on this campaign now, to keep it contained and local."

"Agreed. My boss wants to move on, test this on shaping public opinion."

"And just who is your boss?"

"You don't need to know that just yet."

"It'd help me tailor the message for the right agenda."

Newman pulled out his phone and tapped the screen. "I'll message you an NDA. Sign, then we'll talk specifics."

"This is going to cost your boss a lot more. Absolute minimum 500K."

"Sign first, then we'll talk." Newman waved a hand.

Pedro opened Newman's document on his phone, scanned the NDA, scrawled his signature with his finger, and sent it back. "There. Your collective asses are covered."

Newman steepled his fingers on the table. "All right, then tell me: how would you replicate what you did with this woman—only this time, for something that will have a national impact?"

"That depends."

"On what?"

"On getting the full 500K up front."

Newman unzipped his pack, slid out a thick envelope, and set it on the table. "There's 200 grand in cash here. You'll get the rest—and maybe more—once the plan's set in stone."

Garcia slipped the envelope inside his backpack, struggling to contain his glee. "I can't very well count it in here. I'll shoot you a text once I verify the amount."

Newman tried unsuccessfully to catch the attention of a waiter. Raising his arm, Pedro clicked his fingers: the waiter was instantly at their table.

"By the way," Newman waited until the man had left again, "we checked on this Alice Sinclair's place earlier. Looks like she left town. She's got someone in her life, so odds are she went to see him where he lives and works in Cassadaga."

Pedro let out a dark laugh. "Ah, the Cassadaga—land of the oddball, where everyone thinks they can speak with the dead."

"Well, that's where we'll start."

"Start *what?*"

"Finding her. My boss wants to talk to her."

"Why?"

"Probably to see how this little phenomenon is affecting her. Who knows?"

"I can't see how that's relevant. If I'm doing this job for your boss, the only thing that matters is whether my experiment produces results for them. It is the process, not this Alice woman, that matters. She's a guinea pig. Her time is over."

"Agreed," Newman replied. "But I just pass on my orders."

Pedro rose to leave, feeling a dark thrill surge through his veins. He had just lit a fuse, and now all he had to do was wait for it to blow. His Dream Games had officially begun.

Chapter 9

Back in his luxurious house, Pedro sat in his office on his leather chair, staring at the piles of cash in front of him.

It was lucky that his wife, Leah, was at another of her interminable evening gym classes, and that his rowdy stepsons had finally grown up and left the nest. The 200 grand was an unexpected fortune—but it now was also an anchor binding him to an unseen force he'd just signed himself up for.

He wasn't sure what to do with the money. Depositing it in a single transaction would raise too many red flags—smuggling, trafficking, drug deals. If anyone found out about this, he could lose everything—the book deals, his legions of devoted readers, what was left of his status as an "academic." But did all that matter now? The mountain of money in front of him was far larger than a mere book deal.

It was a means to his glorious end.

He grabbed the first stack of bills and began dividing it. He could stash a little here, a little there, in secret places in the house. No one would be the wiser. One pile went into his old leather satchel, something his father had bought in Havana years ago, an heirloom. A perfect hiding place. Another went into his South American backpack, the one that still smelled faintly of adventure and late-night bus rides through jungles. Maybe that stack could be for something good—a charitable act, perhaps. He could pretend to be the Florida equivalent of the millionaire philanthropist, anonymous but powerful. It seemed ridiculous but perfect.

A small portion could go to furnish the swanky new office he'd been meaning to write his next book in. It was supposed to be his magnum opus, the book that would elevate him entirely out of the academic world and his dead-end university position into a permanent comfortable place where he made the rules.

For years he'd been planning for it. Progress had been slow, but he'd been steadily advancing forward.

But that was the past. His writing clearly wasn't what was going to drive him forward anymore. The real money, the real power play, was in this shadowy game, whatever it was—and whoever was the mastermind behind it.

Jung would have appreciated the synchronicity of it all, he thought. Jung's theories on the collective unconscious seemed quaint now, almost naïve in the face of the raw power Pedro was learning to wield. Jung had built his castle in Bollingen, Switzerland, as a metaphor for the foundation of the human psyche, and Pedro, in his youthful devotion, had traveled and once stood at the foot of the castle, marveling at the concept brought to life in physical reality.

Jung had written about the place in his autobiography, *Memories, Dreams & Reflections*. The four corners of his precious castle symbolized the fundamental parts of human identity: the persona, the anima/animus, the shadow and the self.

Pedro had always been fascinated by the idea that our deepest selves—our hidden selves—could be shaped by the meeting of external and internal forces, that our beliefs, our thoughts, even our realities, were not entirely our own. Jung had often spent time entirely alone in that vast dark castle, where strange experiences had occurred. *Alone in the dark.* There had been power in isolation, in the unknown. Pedro thought now about how he too, was like Jung in his castle, isolated but shaping his external reality. He was using the same power to manipulate perception, to bend reality to his will.

Now Pedro had outgrown his meagre author dream. His next book would never be his greatest achievement, not anymore. The *real* game was here in his digital hands: shaping a new kind of reality, controlling the collective unconscious.

He could be the architect of a new world. The all-knowing puppet master he had always longed to be.

Pedro had always been a methodical thinker, someone who liked control. But now he was acutely aware that this situation, as magnificent in its potential as it was, could also slip from his grasp at any point.

And he must never share his secret method. He could not trust anyone, because once they had his method, he would be of no use to them. And his method was brilliant. The image he had created, that strange woman, wasn't just *seen* in a dream anymore. She was being *felt*, woven into the fabric of the collective mind subconsciously as the *idea* of the stranger, the archetypal unknown. It had taken on a life of its own: she was stepping out of dreams and shadows into reality.

People were even using their Alice nightmares as legal defense when they committed crimes. All this should have shocked him, being responsible for it all, the mastermind. He should be moved to destroy his invention.

Instead, it excited, thrilled, him.

Stacking the last of the cash in his leather satchel, Pedro considered the powerful future he was creating for himself. Ward Newman had been cryptic, but he was clearly involved with someone hugely influential. Someone who wanted power, lots of it—and who was willing to invest boatloads of money to make it happen.

He was a key player in that dream game now. He wasn't just a psychologist or a viral creator anymore. He was bigger—he was a master manipulator of the collective unconscious.

His cell pinged, a text message from Ward Newman. Jung would appreciate the synchronicity.

Have the rest. Can u meet somewhere?

Where?

Bodega on Central and Orange.

Be there shortly.

Chapter 10

Pedro grabbed the iPad that held the hacker-proof schematics for his dream game and carried it out to his car.

The bodega wasn't far, but Pedro decided to circle the block before he parked, making sure Newman wasn't there with cops or federal agents. Given the money involved, and his intuition that Newman likely worked for the government, he sensed the project Newman was going to tell him about might be about an election for Senator, potentially even President. *Don't be afraid to dream a little bigger, darling,* a line from the movie *Inception* came into his head. He laughed out loud. Life really was stranger than the movies.

He thought about the current President's four years in office. His brain started to look for connections, synchronicities. With a series of disastrous decisions domestically and internationally, Jim Shannon's approval rating was at an abysmal 23 percent right now, going into election season. An interesting number.

Back in the '60s, William S. Burroughs, author of *Naked Lunch*, knew a certain Captain Clark who once bragged that he'd been sailing for 23 years without an incident. That very day, Clark's ship had an accident that killed him and everyone else on board. And that night, Burroughs heard on the radio that a plane in Florida had crashed. The pilot was Captain Clark, and the flight was Flight 23. This synchronicity launched Burroughs's number 23 obsession, and he started documenting incidents that involved it.

In the *I Ching*, the ancient Chinese divination system, Hexagram 23 was called *Splitting Apart*. Now that was Pedro's standard for the meaning of the number.

Based just on that 23 in Shannon's approval rating, Pedro suspected the guy wouldn't be reelected as things stood now. Unless there was some big surprise or shift, Shannon was a dead president walking. And Pedro alone could save him!

Even thinking that was intoxicating. The power behind the throne could be his.

He circled the block again. This time he saw Ward Newman seated at a booth at the window of a café, alone. If someone else had accompanied him, of course, they could be at another booth. Pedro wouldn't know for sure unless he went inside.

He drove around to the lot at the back of the café, screening for idling cars, people just hanging out. He didn't see anything unusual.

Hey, am parked out back, he texted.

Be out in a sec.

Where're you parked?

Back lot. VW van, red. Talk in my car.

I'll come to you.

K.

Pedro's eyes swept the lot, scanning for any sign of movement. The harsh floodlights cast murky shadows over the rows of parked cars, but there was enough ambient glow for him to make out four vehicles. Only one of them was a red van. It was tucked in a corner to his left, half hidden by the darkness, its faded paint barely visible in the dim light.

He sat watching, waiting.

Then Newman emerged from the building, walking with a lazy, almost casual gait, a backpack slung over his shoulder, his eyes scanning the lot as he made his way toward the red van. Pedro waited until he had reached the van, then slid out of his own car, his boots making tiny noises on the cracked asphalt. He reached the van and peered through the driver's seat window.

"Figured driving here and meeting in the car was safer," Garcia blurted.

Newman flicked a glance at him before opening the side door. "Definitely. We are safe here. Hop in."

Pedro climbed in and slid into the passenger seat. A sterile smell hit him immediately. The dashboard gleamed under the dim light, uncluttered by fingerprints in sight, the seats perfectly aligned.

Newman tossed his pack into the space between them. "Another 250 grand," he tossed off, as if talking about pocket change. "My boss thought that would make things a little fairer."

Pedro unzipped the bag, taking out a flashlight. The beam cut through the darkness inside the pack. He peered in and the scent of money sent a thrill of pleasure up his nostrils. Cash, all right. Thick stacks of it. He zipped the bag shut. "Can't count it in here. I'll take your word for it."

Newman grunted.

"I've got something for you, too." Pedro pulled out his iPad. The glow of the screen lit up Newman's face for a split second. Pedro brought up a photo of President Jim Shannon; he clicked through a series of images and diagnostics, placing them side by side.

"Here's the thing," Pedro said softly. "This is the President. And this…" He hesitated; had he had overstepped this time? He waited for Newman to stop him and tell him he was wrong; this wasn't about the President's reelection. But Newman's silence was all the permission Pedro needed. "And this is my dreamer's vision of him. The image that is going to make the whole world dream of him when they see it."

Newman squinted at the screen. "I don't know if you're the world's greatest mentalist or a witch. You nailed it—" *Shannon's mouth. Too wide. Too distinct. A politician's smile. It was almost like a signature, a brand, except more insidious. Hypnotic. Compelling.*

"See that?" Pedro tapped the image of Shannon's mouth. "That's not just a smile. It's a subliminal unforgotten message in a shared fever dream." He leaned back, watching Newman's reaction.

Newman took the iPad with a steady hand, examining the photos. He tilted it this way, that way, the light flickering across his face, before he finally handed it back. "This... this is just the start of it?"

Garcia nodded. "What do you think?"

Newman's eyes flicked back and forth between the image and Pedro. "It's good. But proof of the pudding is if it will work. My boss will love it if it does."

"Your boss isn't the President."

Newman's lips twitched. "No, but works for him. Send the image to my phone."

Pedro tapped the screen, then took his iPad back. He studied the other man, waiting for a shift. A tell.

"There's a subliminal message in that image," he blurted. "Do you feel it? Can you sense it? You will dream it."

Newman's phone pinged. "Let me study it again."

Squinting, Newman held his phone up to his nose, close. Then he pulled out a pair of glasses that looked like ones you'd find in a dollar bin at a discount store, their lenses thick.

"What the... have you had cataract surgery recently?" asked Pedro.

"Cataract surgery? Nah, I'm barely 40, man."

"Then what do those ridiculous and ugly and cheap glasses do?"

Newman held up the glasses. "They detect coded subliminal messages in digital images or messages." He squinted again. "But there's nothing here. Can't pick up anything."

"Your glasses are flawed, then. The message is right there. It's clear as day." Garcia flicked through a few other images on his iPad, bringing up the one of Alice Sinclair. "See anything here?"

Newman looked at the screen. "We've already run this image through all our instruments. Nothing's coming up for her. We haven't a clue how it works and why people are dreaming of her."

"The message embedded for her says, 'I'm whatever you want me to be.'" Pedro felt powerful.

"At the end of the day, it doesn't matter, does it really, if the naked eye, spectacles, or dreams can crack your secret subliminal code? The results are clear: your dream game program is working. The hits are up to a zillion and rising. It's genius." Newman looked elated. "By the way, Alice Sinclair's gone. Disappeared. She's on the run. We're on her trail. As I said, my boss wants to meet her in person."

"For what reason? I mean, you've mentioned before that your boss wants to talk with her, but what's the real need?"

"It's her call, Pedro."

Pedro felt a small jolt. "Your boss is a woman?"

"Yeah. You got a problem with that?"

It made sense, in a twisted way. Pedro had read the reports. It had to be President Shannon's right hand, his shadow (or as rumor had it, the woman not his wife that he was sleeping with). A woman who had been with him for years. A woman who had a hand in everything he did. Her name lingered in Pedro's head like a bad omen. "Your boss is Cassandra Mace."

Newman didn't hide his admiration. "Impressive research, Pedro."

He kept his eyes locked on Newman, trying to read him. "If she's putting up this kind of money, she really wants to stay in the game, doesn't she?"

"Wouldn't you?"

The halls of power? Pedro had never been inside them, always an outsider looking hopefully in. But the money Newman was offering him... it was a ticket. A ticket to power beyond even his wildest dreams. "We'll see..."

Newman's hand rested on the briefcase between them. "This money? It puts you at the entrance to those halls, Pedro. You won't be on the outside anymore."

Garcia let the weight of those words settle. "We'll see."

"Okay, so what's the next step for Shannon's image?" Newman was smiling widely. "The boss wants the campaign to start yesterday. What is the subliminal message this time?"

"I am your whole truth." Garcia slung his pack over his shoulder. "That's the subliminal message. It is simple and strong and ticks all the boxes. Everybody wants to know the truth or what is real, and this image will guide them there. When they think of or ask for truth, Shannon is the only answer they will ever get when their eyes are shut and open.

"We start small. One social media site at a time. Test the waters. With Alice Sinclair, the message was simple and obvious, and I deliberately limited its reach. It will continue to flare up now and again, but eventually it will fizzle out when a superior campaign replaces it. She's collateral damage now. With the President... I need a day or so more to refine it, make it stick, make it endure. Ensure it surpasses the Sinclair campaign in every possible way."

"How? You know how to do that?"

Garcia didn't have an answer. "My subliminal formula is perfection," he vamped. "I'm a genius, remember? Your words."

He opened the van door, stepping out into the dark parking lot. It stretched out before him like an endless expanse of possibilities. "I'll be in touch. Tell your Cassandra things are moving ahead from right now. The best is yet to come."

Pedro walked back to his car. In the silence, his engine hummed to life.

The sound of his car driving away was swallowed up by the gathering shadows surrounding them.

Chapter 11

Ward Newman had known it was going to happen eventually.

The night after his meeting with Pedro, a viper-like nightmare of Alice dragged him into a world of bottomless shadows.

He was standing in a cold, empty room when she appeared — a woman with eyes that drilled into him like daggers. One was a sharp, unnatural blue, the other a hollow, mud brown. Her smile twisted into something vile, as though it belonged to a demon, not a person. Her voice slid into his thoughts, a venomous whisper cursing him with words that crushed him. "You are nothing," her tone was drenched in malice. "You are less than nothing."

Suddenly the room seemed to collapse around him. Panic surged as he felt his body betray him — his arms and legs began to shrink, muscles and bones contorting into alien shapes. His skin hardened into something rough and repulsive, and his body twisted uncontrollably, turning into a soft, wriggling mass. He tried to scream, to move, but his mouth betrayed him, only releasing a small, horrified croak. Each second of transformation felt like an eternity, each shift of his body more agonizing than the last. His vision blurred as he became smaller, more vulnerable, terror rising as he realized he was no longer human. He was an alien creature trapped in a body that no longer obeyed him, helpless, some sort of caterpillar. His very sense of self was slipping away, replaced by pure, raw panic. He thrashed, desperate for escape, and the woman's eyes glittered as she watched him writhe, her laughter echoing around him.

Ward woke up at that very moment. The message in the dream was clear: where he was heading there was both terror and transformation waiting.

Chapter 11

Later that morning Ward sat in Cassandra Mace's office, Alice's dream face still weighing heavy on his mind. He stared out the window at Lake Eola in downtown Orlando, watching the usual scenes unfold—joggers, dog walkers, pedestrians glued to their phones, completely unaware of the strange disconnect technology had created between them and the world. What had they focused on before smartphones? The lake, the sky? Each other? How quaint.

"Hi, Newman." Cassandra breezed into the room, the upbeat tone in her voice almost rehearsed.

"Hey, yourself," Newman responded instantly. He was always too eager to please around her. He despised himself for it but couldn't help himself either.

"Diet Coke?"

"Love some. Thanks."

Cassandra was striking, but with an edge—late 40s, brunette, dressed in a cotton pantsuit that was both professional and sharp. Three years ago, she had hired him to be her personal assistant. Her Orlando office was the nerve center of the state's political engine, the pulse of a campaign that had the President's reelection in its sights.

Newman worked long hours; his life entangled with hers almost from the start. He'd become addicted to the excitement, the thrill of feeling important in a way he never had. He'd handled everything from subtle intimidation of political enemies to preparing fake polls that showed the President leading in Florida. He'd even covered for Cassandra's personal life—picking up her daughter for a secret abortion. But today was different.

"Sorry you had to wait." Cassandra set a mug of coffee in front of him. She settled into the chair across from him. "Was the delivery successful?"

"Yes. I've got something to show you." Newman brought up Pedro's image of the President on his phone. He slid it across the table. "He's already started creating the campaign."

85

"Fantastic."

She stared at the image for a long moment. Then reached into her pocket and pulled out a pair of huge glasses to look at it in more detail.

"I can't detect the subliminal message. It's too subliminal" — she pushed the glasses up the bridge of her nose — "which is perfect."

"Honestly, the subliminal stuff isn't the key." Newman winced at her dubious expression. "The guy who created this believes the real genius is not just that he has subliminally coded the image so it will trigger dreams of the President among those with deep-seated pain, hatred, anger or regret, or trauma — and who hasn't got some of that buried inside them, so that's just about everyone isn't it? — but the simple awareness that the President is regularly cameoing in people's dreams. People will hear about this phenomenon and naturally find it intriguing, and then they'll unconsciously set the intention to dream about him. That's the key to dream recall. Telling yourself you want to dream before you fall asleep or just thinking about the possibility of finding meaning in your dreams. And when they do inevitably dream about him, they'll believe he's alive inside them, a part of their subconscious. He becomes *their* American dream. He is inside them. And if they still don't dream about him, they'll feel left out, because everybody else is. FOMO becomes their driving force. Either way, he's percolating in their heads all the time, both when they are asleep and when they are awake."

Cassandra pushed the glasses up her nose again. "Hmm. Still want to know what the coded message is, though. Just in case people only see the picture while they're awake."

"It's simple. *I am your whole truth.*"

She smiled. "How ironic. No spin. I love it. Vague but specific. Nothing and everything."

Newman waited, sensing something more.

"Have you found Alice Sinclair yet?"

"The dream woman? Not yet." Newman said, "May I ask why you want to talk to her?"

"Curiosity," Cassandra said. "How has all of this impacted her life? I haven't dreamed about her and maybe meeting her in person will do the trick. I'm already proving your guy's hypothesis—I'd like to experience what it feels like to dream about her. People I know who have dreamt of her say it is an utterly unforgettable—terrible—experience, but a thrill-ride, too. When they wake up from a dream of Alice, they feel madly alive."

She couldn't possibly understand, could she? Ward thought. Cassandra was the type who'd never pay attention to her dreams, let alone bother with their emotional or subconscious implications. Still, he decided to give her the truth, or part of it. "All I know is that it's completely fucked up her life. She's gone on the run."

"Well, the President won't have to flee, will he? He just needs to infect enough dreams to get reelected."

There's always more with her. "What else, Cassandra?"

She frowned. "I'd like to know if Alice had any inkling about this beforehand. Did she have any dreams? If so, when did they occur? What were they like?"

Newman could almost feel the trap closing around him. "You want to turn her into a guinea pig for the entire campaign. Monitor her."

"Exactly," Cassandra declared. "And I'm curious about something else. Why did the President and some other members of his Cabinet dream that she was a Calypso-like figure drowning them? Why did they have this shared dream? I had to stop myself from laughing when I heard them talking about it the other day. They were like a bunch of old ladies around a watercooler sharing the same dream, shocked expressions on their faces and wildly speculating on the meanings. One of them even started googling."

Newman felt a wave of irritation. "How the hell is she supposed to answer that? She was the guinea pig, remember."

Cassandra's gaze sharpened. "Maybe she consented to it. Maybe she's a double agent."

Newman laughed. "Yeah, right. No one would consent to something like this."

Cassandra tapped her turquoise nails against the table and her black eyes squinted. The blue against the beige wood was jarring, like a warning. "Maybe she did consent. For a price. Everyone can be bought for the right price. That's why you can't trust anyone, unless you're richer and more powerful than them and everyone else in their orbit. What's her relationship with your dream-tech genius guy? Do you know?"

"I don't think there's any relationship at all." Newman had no idea what Cassandra was implying, but the thought of digging into Garcia's private life made him uneasy.

"Maybe the money we've been paying him is money he's been paying her to participate in this campaign. The two of them in it together. Did you think of that?"

Newman felt the blood drain from his face. "I doubt it."

"But you don't know for sure, do you, Newman?"

He bristled, his palms sweating. *This is why she's dangerous.* "Let's get something straight. I did what you asked me to do. I found someone who could create an invisible impossible to detect campaign. So far, he is delivering, but we need to see if it works on a larger scale."

She took a step back, coolly studying him. "In that case, before we pay or progress this further, you'd better find Sinclair so I can speak with her directly. I'm a human lie detector. I'll see if she's lying."

Newman had done her bidding for three years, but this felt different: they were messing with people's heads. Cassandra reached into the drawer of her desk and pulled out an envelope and handed it to him.

The money always spoke louder than anything else.

"Here's 50 grand, Newman. Tax-free. Now go find her and bring her to me, please."

He tucked the envelope into his bag. "I'll do what I can."

Before he'd reached the door, her voice stopped him: "When you find her, bring her to me immediately."

"I should arrest her, is that what you're implying?" he turned to look at her. "I don't have the credentials for that."

Cassandra's smile was icy. "Sure, you do. You work for me. Besides, with this 'a dream made me do it' murder court case catching fire, she needs arresting." She opened a drawer, took out a new ID, and handed it to him.

Newman stared at fake FBI credentials. "I'd be impersonating an FBI agent, which is a felony. And just in case, what dream made me do it?"

"If you'd rather not arrest her, I can have Eric Fitzgerald accompany you," she said. "He's the agent who searched her home. Just wake up and do some research, the dream murder case is everywhere. Where have you been?"

Eric Fitzgerald was a blowhard, a man so incompetent but also so ambitious Newman always felt like he was drowning in the man's shadow.

"I'll do this alone. And I'll get up to speed on the dream murder."

He patted the fake ID in his pocket. "Special Agent Newman reporting. Stay tuned."

Chapter 12

Ward went home first. He needed to figure out what to do with the 50 grand in cash. What had Garcia done with his even bigger wad of money? What was the right move?

The garage door groaned open, only to reveal his wife's Jeep. *Shit.* She was home.

Rachel didn't know anything about this. And he sure as hell wasn't about to explain why he had 50,000 dollars in cash casually tucked into his bag.

He zipped up his pack, slinging the bag over his shoulder, and walked briskly up the long sidewalk. The thick envelope pressed against his side as he tried to think up a believable excuse for where he would be going next.

Work. It was usually enough to get him off the hook. But Rachel had just gotten home. She'd be expecting dinner, a movie, normal evening together. He didn't have time for any of it, no matter how badly he wanted to. Cassandra hadn't set a time limit, but she wouldn't wait long. Impatience was her middle name. He had to move fast.

Rachel was in the kitchen, slicing plantains. He approached her from behind, wrapping his arms around her, his hands resting gently on her swollen belly.

"Make enough for yourself and junior Newman," he said. "I've got to get back to work."

"I thought we could spend some time together tonight." She turned in his arms, sighing. "Did you ever watch *The Devil Wears Prada*? You're in danger of losing your soul to this Cassandra woman."

He smoothed his fingers through her thick ash blonde hair, remembering the last time they'd watched that movie together. "Cassandra has some stuff she wants done."

Rachel rolled her eyes. "Like usual. Hey, I noticed you've been reading a lot of books on dream decoding lately. Midlife crisis? Or is it just the whole becoming-a-dad thing?" She stopped. "You know this strange woman everyone's been dreaming about? I dreamed about her too. Maybe you can enlighten me about the meaning of my dream." She turned back to the stove, flipping the plantains.

"What happened in the dream?"

Rachel added another dollop of butter to the pan. "The two of you were having a steamy affair and she forced me to watch. Ghastly."

Jung would've called this a *trickster synchronicity*—an experience that mocked you, putting you at the center of a cosmic joke. He knew that much from his meeting with Garcia, when the man had gone on and on about manipulating the unconscious to influence decisions. Jung had come up often.

Ward hadn't known about dream analysis then, but he did some research and started to get the bigger picture.

"Why would I do that when I have you, Rachel? Besides, cheating dreams aren't about sex. A dream 'lover' is just an aspect of yourself you want to get closer to. But since I was in your dream, I'm guessing you feel like we need more quality time. I get that. And I'm working on it. As for her, this Alice... What does she mean to you? What's the first word that comes to mind when you think of her?"

"Excitement. Passion," Rachel said. "That's two words. Are you saying I should find a way to get more of that in my life, with or without you?"

"It's your dream, baby. You decide."

"Thanks for the therapy session, *Dr. Ward*. Good Lord, didn't know you were that deep."

Ward watched his lovely pregnant wife finish browning the plantains. She speared one with a fork, holding it out. "Take a bite. See what you think."

It was fantastic—but he needed to go. He needed to track down Alice and bring her in. "Perfect. Save me some," he kissed her lightly. "I'll text you later."

Relief and sadness mingled in him as he walked out the door toward his car. He wanted to keep Rachel out of this mess. His pathetic and inexplicable need to impress both Cassandra and Shannon was toxic, one-sided, and putting everything he cared about at risk. After this job, after this one last job, he'd ask for a transfer. Maybe take some time off. Focus on the future—the future of him as a father, with Rachel.

But just as a precaution, before he drove off, he disabled location tracking on his phone. Rachel wouldn't be able to see where he was now. If she asked, he'd just tell her the phone was acting up.

He glanced back at the house one last time. Invisible strings tugged at him to return, but his mind cut right through them.

Chapter 13

It took Ward less than an hour to track Alice's mobile signal to an unusual address in Gainesville. And less than five minutes to absorb the details of the dream of the Alice murder case and realize more clearly how much the campaign around her had gotten out of hand.

He called Garcia, but the other man didn't seem fazed. He'd already known about the murder case, waving it away, yet more inevitable collateral damage.

If you join forces with a snake, you can't expect them to be anything else than what they are: a snake.

What *did* shock him was Garcia's confession that he couldn't shut down the campaign. Couldn't stop what they had started.

"It's like a virus, Newman. Once it is unleashed, it leaps from person to person. There is no telling where it will end up, or how it will manifest. In biological viruses, they tend to mutate and eventually die out or grow weaker, but I've unleashed a mind virus — at your instruction. I did what you asked and paid for, and it is not within my power to know how this will resolve itself."

"People are killing each other in the name of their dreams," Ward blurted. "There must be a way to shut it down," Ward pleaded.

"Keep your cool — you are as much a part of this as I am now. But if this gives you peace of mind, there might be a way to shut Alice's campaign down."

"What?"

"Replace it with Shannon's. Divert mass attention. People have short attention spans, in both their waking lives and their dreams. They are always eager for their next big fix. Alice's campaign was minimal; it wasn't released to its full potential to infect impressionable minds. But I will make sure Shannon's is.

His campaign will clearly focus the dreamer's mind on him and him alone. With Alice, I still left the dreamer a certain amount of autonomy in their dreamscape and their thoughts. For Shannon, all dreams will lead to him. With everybody dreaming of him, Alice will become a distant dream. Does that make you feel better?

"Alice didn't want any of this to happen to her, but Shannon will bathe in it. And if you are asking how on earth, you and I and anyone else involved, or who we invite in, will be immune from Shannon mania, it's simple. Knowledge of what we are doing behind the scenes, and the fact that it is not natural but artificially created, will protect us. Knowledge is power."

"Rock, hard place, Garcia. How can you be so comfortable with all this?"

"It's who I am, Newman. I'm authentic. I'm not pretending to be noble. This is me. Who are you?"

Ward hung up. Sitting on the bed of his run-down motel, he put his head in his hands. He couldn't go back home to Rachel now. But when the day came that Garcia unleashed this Shannon campaign, Ward would have to find a way to protect her. He would have to tell her to stop dreaming.

Rachel's presence was a reminder of the life he craved but couldn't seem to claim.

Pleasing Cassandra, staying close to the power she offered, was like an addiction—one he knew was toxic, even co-dependent. But despite a growing self-awareness, he wasn't ready to break free, not yet.

The night dragged on, his room a prison of restless shadows, his dreams a jagged mess of fractured realities, silent screams, sagging faces, hair falling out, and nudity. This time Alice didn't appear, but plenty of other symbols of pain, regret, and grief took her place and they all started spinning around and around and around the face of Shannon.

Chapter 13

The next day, taking a private flight to Gainesville, Ward stood at the door of the Grangers' quirky house, his finger hovering above the doorbell. He hesitated a few moments before pushing it.

A dog barked three times, and then a woman answered, her short haircut framing her sharp features. She gave him a cautious look. "Can I help you with something?"

"I'm looking for Alice Sinclair."

As she spoke, a black lab appeared from behind her, its eyes narrowing. It growled, low and menacing.

The woman's hand dropped to the dog's head to calm it. "It's okay, Luna."

But the dog barked again, its teeth glinting in the faint light.

Ward stiffened. He had a long history with dogs, none of it good. When he was a kid riding his bike, a German Shepherd had nearly torn him apart, its jaws snapping at his feet, sending him crashing to the pavement. Only Ward's scream had stopped it.

This black monster was eager to pick up where that damned dog had left off.

He braced for an attack. "Can you control your dog?" The woman bent down, whispered something, and rubbed the dog's ears. The dog turned and sat a few feet behind her, watching him, like a bodyguard.

"Now," she declared, "please tell me why you are here."

He was there to take Alice in for questioning, Ward said, laying out the reasons why. She had no idea where Alice was, the woman told him—just as he expected. All she knew was that her clients were dreaming of Alice. Ward was about to say that he knew she was lying when he heard someone scream, and then a small commotion inside the house.

The woman rushed inside, in haste leaving the door ajar. Seizing the moment, Ward stepped inside.

The body of a young woman with stubby pink and purple hair lay lifeless on the floor. Two men and the woman who had answered the door were crouched around her, and the dog was licking her hands.

She had clearly fainted. Ward's mother had had many fainting spells when he was growing up, so instinct took over as he watched them doing everything wrong as they tried to bring her back. He bent down to check the woman's breathing and her pulse. "Stay calm," he told the others, "get some cushions and raise her legs above her heart."

When her eyes started to blink, he had one of the men cradle her head in his lap and encourage her to sit up.

Ward took a step back, watching for signs of life. Sooner than he'd expected, she was taking a deep breath. Even with the others crowded around her, she looked directly at him.

Her eyes were clear blue, and she looked entirely different. But in that moment, Ward knew that he had found Alice Sinclair, the strange woman of his dreams.

Part Two

Nighttime

Anima/Animus: Carl Jung first described the anima and animus in his 1921 work Psychological Types. They are symbolic representations of the unconscious feminine and masculine archetypes within each person, respectively. They can bridge the personal and collective unconscious, and the goal is to integrate the anima and animus into a well-functioning whole.

Part Two

Nighttime

Chapter 14

Luna stopped barking, but she still trembled, her eyes locked on Ward Newman.

Alice could feel him watching her as Joe helped her get up, making her take deep breaths. *She knew him.* She knew him, but how? Where? When?

Maybe his anxiety around Luna was triggering some false familiarity for her. Dogs often appeared in people's dreams; for dog lovers, the appearance of a dog in a dream was a symbol of unconditional love and loyalty. For those who feared dogs — and clearly, this man Newman was one of them — dreaming of dogs could only be a nightmare.

"Luna, it's okay." Alice turned to the man staring at her. "She's trained to be suspicious of people she doesn't know yet. She won't hurt you, Agent Whoever-You-Are — unless I ask her to. She's my comfort dog. So, if you're taking me in for questioning and don't want me freaking out, it's best she comes with us. You need to face your fear and figure out a way to deal with us both."

"You might benefit from myself and Aisling and Barnes coming along too," Joe urged. "They're notable dream psychologists. Their perspective will be invaluable to anyone who wants to discuss why Alice is traumatizing people in their nightmares."

"The President's communication officer wants to question Alice," Ward commanded. "Not her extended family, complete with dog."

Crossing their arms, the group lined up to block his path to Alice.

Five of them to one of Ward; time to regroup. He texted Cassandra.

Found her. Bringing her in. But she's got company and wants them with her.

Bring her in NOW. Why the company?

They are acting like bodyguards. It's easier if she comes of her own free will.

Who's she coming with?

Boyfriend Sebastian, two dream psychologists sheltering her, and her dog.

???????

Then she was calling him. He moved off so the others wouldn't overhear him.

"Who are these psychologists?" Cassandra hissed. "I want their names."

"Barnes and Aisling Granger."

He heard her tapping away at her keyboard. "Authors. Psychologists. Specializing in dreams. Not much to report other than some minor podcasts and WhatsApp group conspiracy stuff. Okay. They're ineffective. Bring them. Same with psychic medium bullshitter Joe Sebastian."

"That was the plan. We're on our way."

He hung up before she could respond.

The thrum of the chopper's propeller made Alice nauseous; she felt as if she were riding the fastest roller coaster on Earth. Luna lay still beneath her, the thump of her tail against the floor breaking the silence whenever Alice's foot brushed her fur for reassurance, alongside the hasty tapping of keys in a shared chat group.

Alice: *That was surreal.*

Aisling: *I don't trust that communications director.*

Barnes: *The myth fits her name: Cassandra. Could see the future but was cursed. Alice, just be honest about how this has ruined your life. But keep the rest to yourself.*

Alice: *I'd really like to know why she's so interested in me.*

Joe: *Her boss is up for re-election. His ratings are tanking. What if she's trying to use this viral dream stuff and how it's traumatizing people for his re-election? And what's up with Newman, posing as an FBI agent? Isn't that illegal?*

Aisling: *The plot thickens. Bet he knows more than he's letting on. He's been Cassandra Mace's personal assistant for years.*

Newman's voice boomed over the intercom, over the sound of helicopter blades. "Fifteen minutes to landing. Buckle up."

His voice had a strange effect on Alice as she looked out the window. Below, on I-4 and the Florida Turnpike at 3 p.m., the roads were already starting their gearing up to rush-hour gridlock.

The helicopter's blades cut through the night air, a cold wind whipping through the gaps in the fuselage as they descended. A government building rooftop loomed ahead. The chopper touched down with a hard jolt.

Newman slid the door open, helping them each exit the chopper.

As Alice took his hand, she felt an odd pull, unfocused but familiar. Newman was an attractive man, and she felt his noticing her, maybe feeling some pull himself.

The past few months Alice had had a recurring dream of steamy encounters with a blonde, brown eyed stranger. Sometimes she even woke up feeling guilty, as if she had cheated on Joe. Did this mean there was something unfulfilled in her relationship with him? But she had felt closer to Joe in recent days.

Luna pulled her along as they got off the chopper, sniffing the ground in search of a spot on the barren roof to relieve herself.

"No grass up here, girl."

Newman was already striding forward, pointing to a door some yards away. "No time. Let's move. Down to the second floor."

They followed him through a series of deserted, winding corridors until they came to a dark, heavy wood door. Newman gave three sharp knocks, paused, then two more.

"Come in."

Alice's mouth was dry as they entered the light filled office room. Nothing about it was overtly menacing; there were no cameras in sight.

Cassandra stood up from behind her desk and walked toward them.

As she took Alice's hand, the phrase came to Alice: *an unquenchable thirst*. Cassandra flashed a cold smile, swiftly releasing her hand.

"Forgive the pun, but it's a dream to meet you at last, Alice. Thank you for agreeing to see me. Apologies for the unconventional manner. Given the circumstances with this dreadful murder case, we had no choice."

She gestured toward a table by the window. "Make yourselves comfortable, I've ordered some food and drink."

On cue, an elderly woman came into the room, driving a cart laden with platters of food toward the conference table. Pitchers of iced tea glistened under the office's sterile lights as they settled into their seats.

"I understand you are dream psychologists," Cassandra turned to the Grangers. "Had no idea they existed, but here you are. Tell me everything: What's your take on Alice's online image? Is the 'a dream made me do it' murder defense legit?"

"We aren't lawyers," Barnes said choosing to ignore her patronizing tone, "but if you want my opinion, that defense will never pass muster; it sets an unholy precedent. As for the image, it could be any strange woman. Most of us carry an inner archetypal image of a stranger, man or woman. This grew demon wings for Alice because they somehow nailed the specifics and tied it directly to her."

"So just a fluke then? A coincidence?"

Aisling said, "No, it's synchronicity."

"And what exactly is synchronicity?"

"It's when inner and outer events collide in a way that can't be explained by cause and effect, but which has deep personal meaning for the person experiencing it."

"Sounds extremely complicated." Cassandra turned looking unconvinced to Alice. "Does it feel like a so-called 'synchronicity' to you?"

"Hardly, although I understand what Aisling is suggesting. Having said that synchronicity is typically a feel-good term, and that's not how I feel about it. I'm inside too many people's heads at night, and that's a powerful but also a dangerous position to be in. When people meet me, their perception of me has already been formed. I have already traumatized them. They think they know me when they've never met me." *With great power comes great responsibility* the line from *Spider-Man* came into her head. But this wasn't a movie; this was happening.

Cassandra circled the group. "What's your take, Mr. Sebastian? I hear you're as psychic as your mother."

The reference to and awareness of his family background caught Joe off guard. "It's a campaign," he answered. "Some tech experts who maybe watched *Inception* too many times decided to find a way to incubate and infiltrate dreams."

"Campaign for what?"

"To prove it can be done. To prove that the person or people behind this can manipulate people's dreams, that they can control their inner world and, therefore, their perception and the reality that perception attracts. I fear their next move is going to be even bigger."

"Sounds nasty," Cassandra consoled. "Can't let that happen, can we?"

Then she homed in on what she really wanted to ask: "Why do you think some of the President's Cabinet members have dreamt that you were drowning them? Or killing them in unspeakable ways?"

"I don't control how I appear in anyone's dreams, the dreamer does," Alice exclaimed. "But maybe a part of them senses that President Shannon needs to drown in the female vote, or that voters need to feel more empathy towards him as water is often a symbol of emotions. If he wants to win another term, he's going to need more of us backing him."

"Interesting. And not entirely incorrect." Cassandra seemed to be holding something back. "Question: You haven't made an appearance in my dreams. Is that because I don't dream? There must be others like me, right? People who don't dream. What percentage of people don't dream?"

"You do dream. You've just developed the bad habit of not remembering them. Brain scans show we all dream every night — at least five or six times."

"I prefer what I can touch, see, and prove. You know the saying, those who can, do; those who can't, dream!"

"The speed of light. The Periodic Table. DNA's double helix," Barnes announced. "The structure of the atom. The sewing machine. Great music, literature, McCartney's "Yesterday," Shelley's *Frankenstein*, Stephen King's novels... I could go on. All of them inspired by a vision in a dream. Dreams have literally shaped and changed the course of human history, illuminated lives. People have been healed, energized, inspired by their dreams — if only society would stop dismissing them as 'just dreams,' or 'only imagination.' To quote Einstein — the world's biggest dreamer — 'Imagination is more important than knowledge.' We live in a world that values knowledge and logic over imagination and dreams. We need greater balance between the two.

"Dreams are a nightly reminder that we have an inner world, an inner potential that holds vast untapped creativity. The reason you don't recall yours is simple: you don't value them. You don't think about them. But that might change after today.

"You see, the dreaming mind craves attention. What you focus on during the day shows up symbolically, reinterpreted for deeper reflection in your dreams at night. Listen, if you want to dream about Alice, or anything at all, just set the intention before you fall asleep. Tell yourself you'll dream, and when you wake up, you'll remember.

"In those moments between sleep and wakefulness, your mind is highly impressionable. It believes what you tell it. The same goes for when you first wake up—stay still, don't blink, close those eyes, and let the dreams come back to you. And when they do, write them down. Immediately. If you wait, they'll slip away. The stress of the waking world pushes them out, and before you know it, they're gone. According to the Talmud, a dream you don't remember is like a letter from someone who knows you better than you know yourself—and you never read it. Don't let that precious wisdom slip through your fingers."

Cassandra covered her mouth to hide the birth of a yawn. "I wish we had more time to talk about dreams, the universe, everything, but such is life. No time. Busy. Busy. Busy. Thank you for satisfying my curiosity. Alice, you seem to be coping well, and you've got a great team looking after you. Newman will take you back to Gainesville directly. I suggest you keep a low profile until all this dies down. And it *will* die down.

"Oh, and Alice, my dear," she leaned closer, "your disguise doesn't exactly shout 'blend in.' It's more 'look at me' with the horrifying pinks and purples. Woman to woman, I'd have gone for a bleach-blonde rinse. Trust me, if your intention is not to be recognized or to frighten people, you might consider modifying it.

"I believe your homeward-bound chopper is waiting. Newman will keep an eye on you. And best you keep our meeting to yourselves, okay?"

She was done with them, clearly. As she ushered them to the door, Luna stiffened, baring her teeth. A low growl vibrated from her chest.

105

"Your dog has issues." Cassandra complained.

"Nah," Alice tugged Luna away. "She's just a good judge of character."

Cassandra's laugh was forced. "Next time I see y'all, I'll bring dog treats. Believe me and I speak from experience at the end of the day everyone has a price—even dogs."

Newman guided them out to the roof and the waiting chopper.

The group exploded in laughter. "Oh my God, the look on her face," Aisling clutched her stomach.

"Her hands—" Barnes mimicked Cassandra curling her hands to fists at the dog's reaction.

"Good girl." Alice stroked Luna's head. "That was priceless."

"Best not speak about her like that," Newman interrupted. "She's got eyes and ears everywhere."

"Excuse me, Agent—or should I say *Mr.*—Newman," Alice asserted. "She dragged us here, herded us like cattle. For what? To feed her curiosity? Give me a freaking break. We had every right to talk about her like that. We are her equals."

Alice expected the familiar rush of guilt. For once it didn't come; instead, she felt something unfamiliar—a rush of power.

Newman was staring at Alice again; he forced himself to look away. "Go ahead. The pilot will take you to where he picked you up."

The silence on the flight back was thick. Cassandra was toxic—Luna had picked up on that—the kind of person who seemed to belong on top. But only because she was willing to crawl over bodies to get there. The group got busy again on their shared chat group.

Alice: *We need to avoid Ward and Cassandra. Go deeper.*
Aisling: *In what sense?*
Alice: *Into hiding.*

Barnes: *I've got a house in Sarasota. It's under a corporate name. They won't be able to trace us.*

Alice looked at Joe.

Joe: *I think for now she has dismissed us as being a threat—or any use to her. We shouldn't get complacent though. Wherever we go. If she wants to trace us, she will. But Sarasota sounds good. My mom's home is close by—across the state on the east coast of Florida.*

What? He had told Alice his mother's home was north. She tapped his arm, mouthing, *WTF, Joe?*

"Sorry," he whispered. "Back then, I barely knew you. I wanted to keep things minimal. No strings, no identifying details—no relatives to complicate things. You know how it is."

Before? But they'd already slept together by then. Intimacy had been established—and trust. Now he had shattered it.

Alice stuffed her phone into her bag, tears threatening.

When they finally landed on solid ground, Luna strained at her leash again as the chopper left, and Alice unclipped her. "Please don't lie to me again, Joe."

"Shit. I hardly knew you back then!"

"You knew me well enough to sleep with me."

"That's not fair, Alice. It was mutual."

"Yeah? I remember you did a spontaneous reading for me on one of our long debates. I guess you just told me things I wanted to hear."

"You two are exhausted," Aisling interrupted. "Overwhelmed. Save all this crazy couple stuff for later. Let's head to our home now, grab our stuff, and from there, on to Sarasota."

She paused. "And forgive me for butting into something that really isn't my business, but Barnes and I have 28 years of marriage behind us. It has not been perfect, had its ups and downs, but we are still together, so perhaps I've earned the right. Trust me, you can't ever know another person fully.

They can't be perfect for you in every way. Truly, the more expectations you heap on your partner, the more you look to them to complete you or try to control them, the more dysfunctional your relationship will become. The only person you should have expectations for is yourself. Are you two reading me?"

Their argument really didn't matter, Alice thought. Center stage right now—hogging the spotlight, night-light, and all the drama—was the dream virus.

For now, it was still shining directly at Alice.

Chapter 15

The Grangers' back porch was the kind of place where you could lose hours, surrounded by the soft hum of nature: the low wooden fence to the left and right of Alice, and the shimmering lake just beyond. Luna was in her element, darting toward the water's edge, dipping a paw in, and then chasing in frantic circles, racing toward her bowls. Food. Water. A simple ritual in an otherwise chaotic world.

The Grangers had laid out a bottle of wine, glasses, and a tray of sliced fruit and veggies, but it all felt like a mirage. A pleasant breeze kissed Alice's skin, cooling the heat of the day, but the lake's glossy, still surface beckoned her to darker thoughts. If she sank into that water, what would she find: peace, or turmoil? Was her dark vision of drowning a few nights earlier just a prelude to this entire godforsaken mess?

"I like the idea of us all lying low in Sarasota to wait this out so that Alice can be set free," Joe's voice cut through her thoughts. "I think we all need burner phones, so…"

He reached into his bag and pulled out four cheap phones. Alice tried not to show her discomfort; burner phones seemed drastic, and she was still feeling the lie about his mother. Joe's calm was both comforting and infuriating, his inner peace a reminder that she had none.

"We're in each other's directory," Joe handed each of them a burner. "Speed dial's set up. All the phones are equipped with VPNs. No trace—unless Cassandra somehow injected a GPS into us."

Alice cringed at the name.

Barnes interjected, "We need to pack our clothes before we go. Just take the basics."

"So, we can text and talk on these burners without worry?" Alice asked.

"Definitely. Calls, texts—but no emails. And pick a fake name. We're all strangers now."

Alice jumped in first, "I'm Neo."

"Perfect," Aisling chuckled. "Almos. Hungarian for 'dreams.'"

Barnes said, "I'm Strider."

Joe laughed. "Then call me Morpheus."

"We sound like a bunch of movie characters," Alice declared. It felt almost normal, too normal. "Move over, Avengers, the Night Born are here. Gentle academics and their spirit animals, armed only with their superpowers of intuition—sorry, Joe, still can't use the word *psychic*—to save the world."

"No financial info," Joe continued. "No addresses. The phones are prepaid—minutes, texts, data. Once it's gone, we throw them out. Get another."

"Jesus, are you an undercover spy or something?" Alice asked.

A flash of something imperceptible crossed Joe's face.

"Let me show you our hideaway in Sarasota." Barnes flicked open his iPad, turning it so they could all see a house nestled on a hill north of Sarasota, hidden by trees. "One road in, one road out. We've got our own server for the internet. Phones will work on cellular. It's secure. It's just under three hours to Sarasota. The sooner we go, the better."

As everyone rushed to gather their belongings, Alice felt competing emotions rush through her.

This whole Night Born fiasco wasn't just about her. She was the hors d'oeuvre, the appetizer for something sinister, the viral proof that dream manipulation could potentially control and take lives. Whoever was behind this knew exactly what they were doing—and they didn't care who got hurt in the process. She had to stay safe, but she also had to put her dream knowledge to good use and find a way to blow up this whole operation—shut it down.

Luna trotted up, tail wagging, as Alice unlocked Joe's van and dumped her bags inside. Nala trotted right beside her, as if they were deep in conversation. The contrast of them together — the dog so playful and the cat so stoic — seemed like a sign: enemies could work together for the greater good.

Alice took a photo to capture the moment.

They got into their cars — Aisling and Barnes with Nala in her carrier, Luna already hanging out the window of Joe's van, her ears flapping once more in the wind. The world outside felt like it was moving at an unnatural pace. And as they pulled away, heading toward whatever lay ahead, it felt to Alice that everything around her was holding its breath.

And so was she.

Chapter 16

Alice walked through the dense woods, Luna at her side, the ground soft underfoot. The scent of pine and fresh wild roses should have brought her peace. Instead, she was lost in the chaos consuming her since this nightmare had begun.

The days blurred together. St. Augustine, Gainesville, now Sarasota. Had it been only two days—could that be right? She pulled out her own phone from the past life she no longer recognized, which she hadn't dared to touch until now, since Joe had instructed them all to use their burners. But since Cassandra seemed to have taken her eyes off them, it seemed safe to finally check her text messages. Ignoring the dozens still unread, she searched until she found the confirmation she'd sent her department head.

Taking some personal time, she read, memorizing Greta's number to add to her burner phone when her phone pinged with a new text. She snapped it off before it could be tracked.

Greta, she typed on the burner, *sorry I've gone dark. I know this is going to sound totally bonkers, but I've gone into hiding with Joe and some dream experts he knows. Yesterday, we were flown by chopper to be interrogated by the President's communications director, Cassandra Mace. Joe and I did some digging: we think Pedro Garcia is behind this Alice dream program. I think I'm a fucking experiment in a re-election scheme. What would Jung say?*

Greta's reply was swift.

Jung would call this fucked up, girl, but he would adore it too. Run with it. You stay hidden, you hear? College prez got a call from that Cassandra Mace, asking where you are. I told prez you had a family emergency and that's what he passed on to her. That was the day before yesterday. After that, I contacted a friend in the CIA. I'll let you know what I hear now you've made contact. Please stay in touch.

Greta talking to the CIA! Had Alice crossed the point of no return, her beloved career, the first and perhaps only lasting love of her life, now going up in smoke? Alice pressed her fists into her eyes, trying to block out the world, to hold it all together.

Luna was there immediately, whimpering softly, her wet nose nudging Alice's cheek. Alice wrapped her arms around her neck, burying her face in Luna's warm fur.

Clutching the burner, she rose and let Luna lead her through the trees until they reached a small tranquil pond. Alice stood and watched the sunlight play on the water's surface.

Luna wandered to the edge, drank deeply, then sat beside Alice, curling up against her.

The burner phone dinged four times in quick succession.

From Greta:

CIA contact will reach you soon.
Potential bad shit going down with this Administration.
Stay hidden until you hear from her.
FYI: Her name's Griffin.

Luna sensed Alice's distress and flopped onto her back, paws in the air, for Alice to rub her belly. Such a small thing, so powerful, an anchor in the storm.

Alice's phone rang and a woman appeared on the screen, Black, with sharp hazel eyes and a calm demeanour. "Alice? I'm Griffin. Our mutual friend referred me."

"I'm Alice Sinclair, the face of everyone's dreams or their worst nightmare, depending on who you ask."

"And I'm Sally Griffin, but everyone calls me Griffin," the woman said, "I'm with the CIA. Your burner phone is undetected — for now — but I'm now tracking your group. You're likely being hunted."

"What do you do for the CIA?"

"Oh, you know... spy stuff," Griffin said lightly. "I investigate and shut down dodgy re-election schemes before they go public. The undercover ones you'd never ever hear about. Look, let's meet at Sarasota Beach. It's safer if I come to you."

"There's a café I know well by the water called Havana." Alice replied.

"There in an hour. I'm in Fort Myers right now—about 80 miles away."

Alice felt something new stirring as the woman hung up: the call from and into the unknown. And a faint flicker of hope.

Sarasota Beach had been one of Alice's favorite Florida escapes as a teenager. Six islands, each with its own stretch of golden shore, nestled on Siesta Key. The Havana café had become a staple of her routine whenever she visited.

But the recent storms had changed everything. They had savaged the region. Homes were reduced to splinters, buildings drowned in floodwaters—no matter where Alice looked, she saw destruction. Yet amid the chaos, somehow the café and other shops along the beach had managed to maintain a semblance of normalcy.

Could Alice do the same?

Alice and Luna entered Havana through the beachside entrance. Joe and the Grangers settled some distance away at a table near the railing, with a clear view of the horizon.

A teenage server approached Alice, dressed in the café's uniform: shorts, a soft blue T-shirt with "Cafe Havana" emblazoned across the front. "What can I get for you?"

"Water for my dog and a lemonade for me."

The server smiled, glancing down at Luna. "She's gorgeous. What's her name?"

"Luna."

"Love it. Like my favorite dreamy character in *Harry Potter*. Water and lemonade coming right up."

It never failed to amuse Alice how people always seemed more interested in knowing Luna's name than in asking hers. When she looked up from the menu, an imposing Black woman in a sky-blue suit stood on the other side of the railing. She folded her arms, her eyes locking onto Alice.

"Griffin?"

"Alice?"

Alice gestured toward the empty seat. "Join me."

Griffin laced manicured unpainted fingers together on the table. She wore a simple but polished look—elaborate dreds hanging over each shoulder, a touch of mascara, a whisper of lipstick. Late 40s, Alice guessed.

"So now what?" Alice said. "I know squat about the CIA, aside from what I've seen at the movies and the spy stuff you're doing, which I don't understand seems to be against the President."

"My contract is with the U.S. Constitution, not with the President, Congress, or Senate or any party," Griffin said. "I believe President Shannon, like most presidents before and no doubt after him, is involved in unethical activities intended to subvert the next presidential election. I'm not the only one who thinks so, though we have no proof yet. But whispers abound. And in my experience, where there's smoke, there's fire."

The server arrived with their drinks. "I think I was their preliminary test," Alice said once she'd left.

"And it was successful," Griffin said. She twirled a dred around her finger, then flicked it over her shoulder. "And now it's deadly, with the murder case implicating you, dreams of you, in its defense. Imagine if people start having shared dreams where you encourage them to commit crimes collectively? It's got to be stopped, and fast.

"We believe—but have no proof—that they may have hired the same election person to create a dream-hacking campaign to get Shannon reelected. That's potentially interference, because when people view the image, they don't know their minds are being messed with. But this is how authoritarian governments work, Alice. They evolve, just like technology. And they're digging deeper than ever. It is not enough anymore for them to get everyone seeing them everywhere and talking about them. They want to get inside us, invade and control the intimacy and privacy of our inner space, our nocturnal dreams, the last truly independent space within us. I'm telling you, nothing like this existed a few years ago. They aren't content with daytime dominance over our thoughts and what we see and hear; they want to possess our nights, and our dreams too."

"How can I help? What do you need from me?" Alice asked.

"Details. Dream details. Ways for us to understand how this attack works, so we can block it. Kill it before it gets out."

"Then we need more dream experts than me on the case." Alice called Joe and the Grangers over, pulling out chairs. "My Night Born team. Because big dreams are born in the night. Their superpowers are dreaming analysis, intuition, compassion, and a burning desire for equality, freedom of dreams, and inner peace for all."

Griffin smiled with recognition as Joe arrived. "Sebastian, your mom's undercover work is legendary in certain circles. She's done remote viewing for us—sensing things beyond the scope of normal human perception." She turned to Barnes and Aisling. "And if I'm not mistaken, you've worked undercover for a couple of government agencies as well, haven't you?"

Alice gasped, "You two never mentioned that."

"Couldn't," Barnes replied. "NDAs. Despite what everyone's been told, the Stargate program, government-funded psychic operations, hasn't fully shut down. Don't get me started on what the government knows about UFOs."

"We need your help now for a danger that is clearer and more present," Griffin said. "The threat is not from outer space, but from our inner space. Some of us in the government have intercepted messages suggesting that President Shannon intends to disrupt the election in November by any means necessary. Right now, his approval rating is abysmal, so it is possible he's enlisted Cassandra to experiment with a viral dream-hacking campaign. You know everything there is to know about dream research. Who do you think she hired for this project?"

"We suspect it might involve a psychiatrist called Pedro Garcia. Who I may have a connection to that he doesn't suspect. My mother had a brief fling with him decades ago in her student days. Nothing serious, but enough to get the measure of the man."

Griffin scrolled on her phone. "Psychiatrist, famous dream author, and media expert. Married an American woman, Leah Church, former Miss Florida. They live in Orlando, and he keeps a second residence in Gainesville. She works part-time for a high-end ethically sourced perfume company. No kids, but two stepsons. Born in the U.K. Holds dual citizenship. Shoot. He's traveling to the U.K. first thing tomorrow for a Raven Bookshop signing event the day after."

"It's the place to be if you're a New Age author," Joe said; he'd done a few talks at the store himself. "So, the traitor is just carrying on and living his dream and doing a signing or workshop there."

Griffin was staring at Alice. "I dreamed of you too, but your eyes looked different."

Alice did her now habitual reveal.

Griffin said, "My oh my! It's really you. I was running from you in my dream, but I couldn't get away. The ground beneath me kept shifting, pulling me in. It felt like the sand was alive, twisting and tightening around my legs, sucking me deeper with every step I took. The harder I struggled, the faster it pulled, and I could feel it reaching up, creeping over my chest, suffocating me. I screamed, but no one could hear me. I have never felt so completely alone and trapped, unable to escape."

"Classic anxiety scenario," Alice said. "It's cathartic. In a tough line of work, you need the release that nightmares can offer. You feel the panic and confusion in the dream state, so you don't have to go there in the day. You can be more clearly focused on the task at hand when you're awake."

"Hmm. That's sort of helpful. But do you want to do more than just dream analysis?"

"Yes!"

"Okay, I want all four of you to go to the U.K. and attend Garcia's talk. You'll blend right in—you are his target audience, speak his language." Griffin said, "Fire him with questions about dreams he'll love to answer. Flatter him, if need be, to see if he reveals anything that can help us shut this operation down.

"Make sure you record everything he says. We need data. If money is his thing, we've got that. Tell him he needs to be on the right side of history. You speak his language. He's likely extremely clever and good at reading people, and he'd suspect our agents in a moment and clam up.

"Everything's falling into place. You will be assigned a private plane, plain-clothes bodyguards, safe house locations, and wired up with recording devices all the way. Now I understand we have, in this unusual band of brothers and sisters, what? Three psychics?"

Aisling's eyes glinted. "We all work differently. Joe's the one with the real gift. He's a natural-born precog."

"I don't know about that," Joe's voice was a little too loud.

"When I was about 13 or 14," Griffin said, "I found a 1956 issue of *Fantastic Fiction* with a novella by Philip K. Dick—*The Minority Report*. My mom was into sci-fi, and she used to hoard old magazines. How does it work for you?"

"I don't need to float in a pool with tubes and wires," Joe protested, "but yeah, being a precog has its perks. Alice calls it highly developed intuition."

"Good to know. And you, Aisling?"

"I'm a psychometrist."

Barnes explained, "She picks up on information through objects people touch."

"Psychometrist," Griffin tested the word. "I see. And Barnes? How do you work?"

"I read energy fields. It's like sensing the vibe of a place, a person, a situation. It's all about the energy around them. I use my sixth sense. It's an intuitive sense we all have, you know—we've just forgotten how to train and how to trust it."

"So, in theory, you all are super sensors and gather different pieces of the puzzle in invisible ways. What are you all sensing about our situation, our chances of success?" Griffin said. "What's really going on? I need specifics. The problem I have when I work with intuitive people is that everything always sounds so vague and, well, general."

Barnes shifted. "It *is* vague and uncertain because life is uncertain. Everything depends on the choices we make in the present moment. The power of now."

"So, what are you sensing now?"

"That Cassandra's sending someone to track Garcia too. She doesn't trust him. She likely sent Ward Newman. A man who loves to be close to power. But I'm sensing he hasn't got the appetite to own that power."

Joe jumped in. "But that version of Newman might be wearing thin. Sometimes people outgrow the roles they play. It's like clothes that no longer fit. He's got potential for both good and bad, but we can't know for sure until the moment arrives. I've said it before, and I'll say it again: understanding a person's personality is one thing; predicting their actions is another. In the end, emotions drive people, not logic. That's why practices like meditation are so powerful—they help us detach from our emotions so we can observe and understand them better, learn and grow from them rather than just react to them. And as for precognition, this isn't an exact science. Sometimes the connection, like the internet, just... drops."

In this dream game, not even psychics with proven credentials could predict the outcome, Alice thought. But their brave new future had been set. The wheels were in motion.

The safe house Griffin had arranged felt like it was buried deep in the heart of a vast, oppressive forest, though Joe couldn't quite pinpoint which one. Barnes navigated the dirt road, passing scattered homes with long private driveways. They hadn't driven long enough for Ocala National Forest. This wasn't the wilderness, just a secluded rural neighborhood, swallowed whole by a vast canopy of trees.

"Your destination is 200 feet ahead on your right," the GPS voice broke in.

Barnes veered off the road, tires crunching against gravel as their headlights fell on a dark SUV parked near the house. Two men stepped out of it—imposing figures in black suits, silhouetted by the faint light.

Barnes rolled down his window.

"I.D.s, please," the first man requested, voice low.

They handed over their driver's licenses. "You want the dog's tag?" Alice asked.

The second guard cracked a smile. "What's her name?" Despite the tension Luna wagged her tail, always eager for a new friend.

"Luna."

"We're good here." The first guard handed back their I.D.s. "If you can pull up alongside the SUV..."

They piled out of the car, Luna's paws light on the soft ground. Once the guards had dropped their formal tone, they began to warm up, seeming almost friendly. The younger one, Chico, was Colombian, dark-eyed, and fluent in English. He knelt and spoke to Luna in rapid Spanish. Luna extended an eager paw. Chico laughed, taking it. "Un placer, Luna."

The second guard, Matt, was a blue eyed all-American and solid, with a broad chest and a quiet strong vibe suggesting he had seen and lived through too much. "Grab your stuff, make yourselves at home. The house is prepped and ready to go. Chico and I will be out here watching all night."

The house was warm and inviting, almost too cozy, given the circumstances. Soft lamps illuminated each room, casting long shadows against the curtains, which were drawn. Simple comfortable furniture created a space designed to soothe nerves.

The fridge was stocked with a week's worth of supplies. A basket of fresh fruit sat on the table, alongside four bottles of wine. The coffee machine was already primed, anticipating their arrival. Luna's bowls were filled on the floor.

Alice and Joe wandered down the hall, dropping their bags on the bed. The room was neutral, made to blend in rather than stand out. The private bathroom was stocked with everything they'd need: fresh towels, soap, and shampoo.

Alice fell back on the bed, throwing her arms out at her sides. "This place is a perfect refuge. And I bet this bed doesn't squeak."

"Let's find out," Joe said.

The bed might not have squeaked, but they did. Still, Alice felt like she was going through the motions. She only saw her dream stranger's face as they made love, even though Joe was perfect, at peace with himself.

Why was she not feeling it?

After, Alice turned her head on the pillow and saw Luna watching. "It's okay," Alice patted the bed. "You can come up with us now."

Luna jumped between them.

"She understands you," Joe laughed.

"Can you communicate with animals?"

"I've never tried. But sometimes I pick up what they're feeling. It seems to be random."

"So, what does Luna feel about all this?"

"I think it's along the lines of 'I will defend all humans who love me and treat me with kindness.'"

Alice's burner dinged. She stretched over the side of the bed to pick it up. "Text from Barnes. *Breakfast whenever everyone wakes up. I'll cook. We feel safe here.*"

So did Alice. She considered getting up to write in her red journal, but her head sank deep into the pillow. When Joe reached for her hand, Alice had already fallen asleep, her arms wrapped around herself.

Chapter 17

Their late breakfast was simple but filling: Barnes had made pancakes, eggs, toast, and crispy hash browns. He had invited Chico and Matt, and Aisling had whipped up fresh espressos for everyone, laying out a platter of delicate pastries. Flavoured dog biscuits and water waited for Luna when Alice gave the command.

"Why do you make her wait for food like that?" Chico asked.

"When she was a pup, I lived next door to a guy who hated dogs," Alice said. "Luna could sense it. Whenever he walked past, she'd fly down the driveway, barking like she was ready to tear him apart. One day, he screamed at me, saying he'd take matters into his own hands. I was terrified that he'd throw poison over the fence, or worse. I trained her to wait for my command before she ate anything."

Chico spoke next, "People like that... they're missing souls. Just like the guy behind this viral campaign that's turning your world upside down. Evil in his blood."

"It's both nurture and nature, when it comes to character," Aisling cut in. "The decision to choose evil is one the individual makes for themselves." And while she was speaking Alice couldn't help thinking, was she her father's daughter? A natural-born cheat and liar? She had just been dreaming of another man when Joe made love to her.

Joe yelled, "Oh my God, Alice. There's a new dream campaign in town. You're old news. Look at this." He held up Shannon's image on Instagram with its surge of likes and comments. "Only seems to be on Instagram right now. No sign on TikTok."

"That's where it started for me," Alice interrupted. "But it will likely spread like wildfire across every platform. Soon, the President will push it to TV, radio, podcasts—anything that can be used to get inside people's dreams. The only positive is the night-light might just move away from me now and I can come up for air."

Chico looked afraid. "I don't want him in my dreams. Don't want to wake up with him on my mind. He's a... a corrupt man. He wants to deport people like me."

"We're all going to stop this." Alice spoke with calm conviction, "I don't know how, but together we can defeat this."

A call came on her burner: Griffin. Alice went outside, the cool air hitting her skin as Luna darted outside past her. The backyard garden stretched out in front of them, a fountain gurgling in the center.

Alice eyed the two men standing at the garden's edge watching her. "I like these two you've assigned us. Thanks."

"Chico was meant to be one of President Shannon's Secret Service agents, but the man couldn't stand anyone who wasn't his own shadow, so he fired him. Matt's been with me for over a decade. Salt of the earth."

"They joined us for this huge breakfast Barnes made." Alice watched Luna circle, chasing her tail.

"Good. Glad you've eaten, because just got word that Pedro Garcia and his wife are on their way to the U.K. Matt and Chico will get you to the nearest private airstrip. You all need to leave shortly."

"What about Luna?"

"She's good to go. Just show her vaccination certificate when you land. Everyone's cleared. Except for the cat. We'll keep her safe here. Hope you've got your passports updated."

"We're good." Alice paused. "What does this make us, contractors?"

"Exactly. You're now part of the Night Born dream team."

"Whose team?"

"The good guys, of course. The light side of the force."

"I hope it's okay that my mom might join us in the safe house when we get to the U.K. She might have useful details to share about her time with Pedro. You can trust her—she knows about everything going on with me and is sworn to secrecy."

"If you've spoken to her already, it's out of my hands. But categorically no more sharing with anyone. Trust no one with what you know outside of this circle of trust. Okay?"

Alice sank into a chair by the garden fountain as Griffin cut the call, texting her mother.

Prepare to suspend your disbelief: I'm coming to London on a private flight tonight. Don't know the exact time yet, but I'll text when I do, and where I'll be staying.

Private flight?? That's got to cost.

Not paying, they are. We're all contractors for the CIA now, Joe and the Grangers and me. And Luna's with us too!

So, you'll be the fantastic four—five if you include me—plus pooch. Are you sure you're not kidding me?

Never been surer in my life. Trust you to tell no one. Luv u.

Ditto. Will this message self-destruct in ten seconds ☺

♥

Alice watched Luna tear around the yard, oblivious to what was about to unfold. Then she returned to the house, where everybody was already packing.

But it was not enough to just try and unsettle Pedro, Alice thought as she packed. In the bathroom as the shower ran, she called Griffin.

"Alice? You guys good?"

"I need a task, something specific. Something I can do. We can observe and try to crack Garcia, but what if he doesn't break? I need more, a mission that ends Shannon's viral campaign."

There was a pause. "Get his laptop, his iPad if you can—whatever he's using to run those mind-control algorithms. Chico and Matt can help. Garcia won't suspect anything, so he may leave his device unattended at the talk. Or get his fingerprints if he does a book signing."

"Got it." Alice was tired of just observing, passively being dreamt about. Now at least she could do something more practical.

The rest of the group was already heading outside when she'd finished showering and dressed. Joe was sitting in a chair waiting for her. He got up when she came in and took her shoulders. "If we don't stop this dream campaign, Shannon wins a second term. That's what my gut tells me. His face is everywhere, on every screen; soon it will be in everyone's dreams and when that happens there is no going back for the U.S. and the world.

"They're not just voting for him; they're being controlled from inside out and outside in. And when the autocrats, the dictators from every corner of the world, start calling, looking for a seat at the table, it won't only be about power—it will be about the secret to everyone's dreams. Pedro sells his dream-hacking formula to the highest bidders—the Saudis, the Iranians, the North Koreans. Every goddamn dictator in the world. They walk away billionaires, and the rest of us get herded around like cattle."

Alice put her arms around him, resting her head on his chest. "I love you," he whispered.

Alice had heard those words in a dream—they'd felt darker, more urgent, more *hers*. She hated herself for wanting what Joe couldn't give. "Ditto," she whispered despite herself.

Her mind went to Griffin and the new purpose the agent had given her. Alice would undo the damage Pedro Garcia had done to her and to her mother—and maybe stop the entire world falling under the sway of a new tyrant.

She was going to find her father. She would come to know him. And know herself, for the first time.

Griffin fist-bumped each of them as they boarded the private plane. "Make yourselves comfortable. We'll be airborne soon."

Alice wanted to ask a question—several—but once they were in their seats a flight attendant interrupted to say, "I had a dream about you. I dreamt we were doing The *I Ching*.

The *I Ching* had always had a strange pull for Alice. When she was younger, she had studied the ancient divination system. "What was I doing in your dream?"

"I was standing in a shadowy temple, surrounded by the symbols of the *I Ching*. You were there, and you urged me to cast the hexagrams. But when I did, the symbols morphed into grotesque pleading faces."

Could this be a sign? It was like the Tarot reader's nightmare. Ever since she'd first encountered Jung's writings on synchronicity, Alice had been a believer. But to hear someone mention the *I Ching* now, here, felt too real. Too timely.

"What hexagram number did we draw?"

"Number 11. So, although the dream was scary, it was a sign of great hope."

"How so?"

"In my culture," the flight attendant said, "we believe numbers are energies, messages from the universe. For us, 11 is a master number, a symbol of new beginnings. A doorway opening. An auspicious sign. Green shoots from infinity. Illumination is coming."

The timing felt uncanny. The number 11 had been following Alice around for weeks, whenever she checked her watch and elsewhere, trying to tell her something—even before all this dream hacking turned her life upside down. "Thank you," Alice replied.

The flight attendant bowed her head, then moved on. Alice glanced at her watch and wished she hadn't. 11:15.

She'd missed it. Four minutes too late.

Was the moment gone? Or was it still waiting for her?

A hum vibrated through the plane's walls, then a thud. The lights flickered, and the seat belt signs flashed and beeped.

Alice needed to buckle up.

Chapter 18

Another sleepless night, another rundown motel. The steady light of Pedro's screen kept him focused as he honed the President's image—slick, precise, calculated—and the underlying schematics of his formula.

The message this time was simple, in plain sight. "Can you identify this man? Have you met him in your dreams? First correct answer gets a $100,000 prize."

Pedro hit upload, using an alias account, then stood and poured himself a celebratory glass of wine. His paced the room: in a day or a week tops, the Shannon campaign would go global. He would be out of the country by then, attending a high-profile bookshop signing in central London. No one would trace the image back to him. *Genius!*

He couldn't wait to monitor the campaign overseas. Perhaps the media would ask him to offer his expert take as one of the world's leading dream experts. He would be a natural over FaceTime, with London Bridge as his backdrop.

His wife, Leah, accompanying him gave him an even better cover. He was the perfect husband to the perfect wife, a former beauty queen who loved to spend his money but knew when to give him space. In 20 years of marriage, she'd never once questioned his need for distance; he'd never seriously questioned her loyalty, except once but it been something and nothing.

Leah had been married before; her two boys lived abroad now. Pedro saw them a handful of times a year. He'd never wanted kids, happily left the parenting to her. A perfect arrangement.

Seventeen minutes in, Pedro refreshed the Instagram page; the post already had thousands of likes. Alice's campaign had moved a bit faster.

He snapped a screenshot and texted it to Newman. *Working already. Should I expand to other social media sites?*

Incredible, the reply came. *Let me send it to Cassandra first. She'll want to see this.*

For the next hour, Garcia tweaked the image and its message, reshaping them so they'd be ready when he got the go-ahead to send it out to every other corner of social media. He'd hit the dark web later.

Full speed ahead from tomorrow, Newman texted just as Pedro was finishing. *Cassandra's impressed—never easy to do that. She says if he's re-elected, there's another bonus in it for you—up to a million. So, onward, amigo. Sky's the limit.*

For you, maybe, Pedro thought, *amigo*. For him the sky was just a starting point. He had infinitely bigger plans.

The light of a new day bled through the blinds by the time Pedro stumbled home. Leah was at the gym again, so he booted up his desktop, searching for flights. Orlando to London, first class. This was his chance to leverage every ounce of fame and influence he had. Far away, clearly nowhere near the dreams of Shannon, he'd sit back and watch his vision play out. He needed Leah there, and his adoring mother, for the photo ops, applause, admiration.

Just as he thought of his mother, a text from her came on his phone:

Hi love. What's your take on this viral image of the woman everyone's dreaming about?

It's happening in the UK too?

Sure. I dreamed about her and so did three of the women in my book group. There were a couple of pieces about it in the press.

Wow. What was she doing in your dream?

Schooling me in Jungian theory. At least, that's what I think it was. Something about archetypes and the collective unconscious. That's Jungian, right?

Why was this Alice woman appearing in his mother's dreams? He hadn't predicted an overseas uptake. Had the expansion diluted things? Why was Alice suddenly educating and not terrifying people in the dream?

Yes, Jungian. I want you to do something special for yourself. I'm sending money through PayPal. Use it to come to central London and attend my talk at Raven Metaphysical Bookstore on Tuesday. Booking details online.

Sweet of you, but not necessary to send money.

As his screen flashed a notification for the transfer of three thousand dollars, he added another twenty grand, the amount he'd deposited into his account yesterday.

My God, are you dealing drugs now or something?

Nah. Got a lucrative side gig that's been keeping me super busy.

Looking forward to seeing you at Raven. And you know, my love, you can always come and see me here anytime. It doesn't always have to coincide with work.

Sending her a string of heart emojis he didn't feel, he checked the progress of his Shannon campaign. The world was watching. And Pedro was going to make damn sure they never looked away again.

Chapter 19

Ward and Cassandra touched down in D.C., heading for her Georgetown townhouse as the afternoon sunlight spread heat over the city. Ward took in the familiar cobblestone streets: the eclectic mix of trendy boutiques, quiet cafes, historic stone buildings. The city felt like it had been here for centuries—but there was an impermanence to it, as if it were a place where secrets were easily buried.

Cassandra's townhouse was comfortable but devoid of warmth, more temporary refuge than home. No personal touches: anyone could live here. "The President is coming *here*?" Ward said.

"That's what he chose to do. He's got a thing for incognito recently—sunglasses, a big hat, even a wig. It gives him a sense of freedom, I think." Cassandra turned toward the kitchen. "Grab a chair. I'll bring coffee."

The small park across the way seemed innocent enough. Out the window, Ward could see a couple stroll by with their dog on a leash. Taking out his phone, he opened Garcia's message, and the file attached to it: *Impressive numbers on IG. TikTok and global domination next. Will be in touch.*

Ward showed Cassandra his screen when she returned with steaming mugs. "Stellar numbers. In less than 12 hours."

Cassandra glanced with admiration at her phone as it buzzed. "He's on his way up."

Two men in plain work shirts, baseball caps pulled low over their brows, stepped into the room. Ward didn't need to be told who one of them was: the President of the United States. Jim Shannon wasn't exactly incognito; he had the presence of someone who'd learned how to command a room.

He looked uncomfortable—too tall. His broad shoulders hunched slightly as he tried to blend into the background, but his height and his wide mouth gave him away.

The muscular short man beside him was Shannon's long-serving Secret Service agent, Roger. Armed to the teeth, he locked eyes on Ward.

"I'm not armed," Ward blurted, holding up his hands.

"It's fine, Roger," Shannon said. "He's with Cassandra. Helping me get re-elected. He's one of us." Hugging Cassandra, he shook Ward's hand, a too-perfect smile stretching across his face. "Such a pleasure to meet you, Ward."

Only his wife Rachel called him that. It should have felt thrilling; the President of the United States had used his first name. Instead, it somehow stripped him of his identity.

At 70, Shannon looked barely 50. He was better-looking in person, with a strong jawline and impossibly blue eyes even his enemies must fall into. He exuded charm. "Well, what've you got for me, Ward?"

Ward pulled up Garcia's screenshots. First, he showed Shannon the success of Alice Sinclair's experimental campaign, its skyrocketing numbers on countless sites. Then he pulled up the Insta numbers for the President's budding campaign. They had climbed fortuitously again.

Shannon scrolled through, stopping now and then to read comments. "Listen to this: *Me and Shannon. We watched an old movie in my dream*—Gladiator. *He threw me to the lions and then beheaded me.* And this one: *He read the Bill of Rights, then laughed at me and ripped it up.*"

"Both dream hero and nightmare villain," Cassandra said. "Love how unsettling this is for their minds. The more chaotic their thinking, the more they need us to tell them what to think. Besides, no such thing as bad publicity, right?"

"What about other sites?"

"The guy we hired is working on uploading to the others. I think he tailors the images to fit each social media platform."

"How?"

"I'm not the tech expert. It's his unique dream-hacking formula."

"That puts him in the driving seat, never good," Shannon said. "I'd like to meet this man. Be assured of his loyalty. Can you arrange it? He needs to be watched and contained. Get leverage, something dirty on him. People are rarely what they seem; there are always skeletons. I need to own what's inside his head."

"I don't think that's necessary," Cassandra said. "We've got Newman on him, watching his every move."

"It's very necessary," Shannon barked. "You and Newman arrange the meeting. I want him here and eating out of the palm of my hand. The sooner, the better."

"It would be more under the radar to corner him in his hometown, Orlando."

"Fine. Roger will fly me to Orlando, and we'll go see this shrink in person. It'll be a private visit. You two find out if Garcia's in town, and I'll pay him a visit incognito."

As abruptly as he'd entered, he was gone.

Cassandra turned to Ward. "So, what do you think?"

"Let's keep it simple. Get Garcia and the President in the same room. We have some loose ends—Alice, Sebastian, the Grangers. They may be suspecting something is afoot that we've got a hand in. Should I continue to track them?"

"Low-key surveillance," Cassandra said. "You're right, they know far more than they should, but trust me, they are not a threat. Haven't got it in them to do anything but talk and dream. Garcia is the challenge. Don't lose sight of him. He's getting hungry off his sense of growing power, which makes him a threat. We need to be one step ahead of him. And we won't need him once we've charmed, wined and dined him enough so that he willingly gives up his formula."

Ward reminded himself never to become her enemy.

Three years ago, when Cassandra had hired Ward, the President had seemed like a breath of fresh air, an agent for positive change who would walk their talk. The smile, the charm, the perfect pitch. It had sucked Ward in, made him think that maybe there was a chance for something better—and he could become a part of it, make a difference.

Then Shannon had shown his true colors. Gradually at first, then rapidly as the years rolled past. Four years of promises of policies that did nothing but fatten the wallets of the super-rich. What had Shannon done for people like him? For anyone who wasn't swimming in cash.

Lower taxes? Equality for all? A joke. Safer streets, cheaper education, cleaner water, safer food? None of it had touched the lives of the people who needed it most.

Ward closed his eyes. Out of nowhere, Alice's face inexplicably came into his head. Alongside all the growing rage.

Why did he still feel bound to Cassandra? To the role his job, his President, and his government had assigned him to. All his life Ward had obeyed orders from those democratically elected to be in authority, in good faith. And Cassandra expected unquestioning devotion.

But it was becoming harder, with Alice stuck in his head and in his dreams like an unforgettable song playing on a loop.

Chapter 20

Pedro was in bed with Leah when his cell phone rang. Thankfully, Leah was out cold; she'd overindulged in wine at dinner.

He padded into the bathroom, shutting the door.

"It's Newman. We need to meet ASAP."

"You've got to be kidding. It's after midnight."

"We're at Cassandra's sister's house—next neighborhood over."

Pedro recognized the address—a strange coincidence. "I hope you and Cassandra know I don't really know jack about how this viral dream campaign works, all I know is that it works."

"Of course you do. You created the whole thing. You're the mastermind. The President wants to see what you've got. Bring your balls and whatever else you need."

"I'm guessing I don't have a choice."

Pedro dressed quickly. Then he had an impulse to call Newman. "How about some bloody honesty? What's this cloak-and-dagger meeting all about?"

"It's simple. You know me, you know Cassandra. You're the connector."

The word didn't sit right.

"You're less than five minutes from me. All will make sense then," Newman cut the line.

Pedro stalked back to the bedroom, his phone's flashlight cutting through the darkness as he pulled on his Skechers. He couldn't wake Leah, so that meant no car; the garage door creaked.

There his bike was in the hallway—fast, quiet, perfect.

The night was dense with shadows, bursts of moonlight illuminating the street as he pedalled toward Cassandra's sister's house.

Two Secret Service agents emerged from the shadows as he reached the gate, flashlights cutting through the darkness.

"I.D.?"

"I'm Pedro Garcia."

"Uh-huh. I.D. NOW."

Pedro handed the taller agent his driver's license.

The agent snapped a photo and handed it back. "What's in the bag?"

"Nothing that's going to bite." He passed the bag over, and the agent scanned it quickly.

"Ms. Mace and Mr. Newman are inside, waiting for you."

They patted him down for weapons, and Pedro stepped inside to see the President seated at the head of a round mahogany table. Ward Newman was to one side. Cassandra sat opposite.

A younger woman, taller, blonder, and softer than Cassandra, appeared, setting a place for him.

"Welcome, Mr. Garcia," she said. "I'm Juliana, Cassie's sister."

President Shannon stood, offering a firm handshake. "Thanks for coming at this godforsaken hour, Pedro."

"No problem, sir." *Big problem, sir.*

Pedro poured himself iced tea and took some food, dazed. Cassandra passed out special glasses.

Newman shot him a look. "You finished it yet? Show the President what you can do."

"Filtering into Instagram," Pedro took out his iPad, tapped the screen, then turned it so everyone could see. "Ready to upload fully and then globally to Facebook, TikTok, X, and Substack. Those four give us potentially billions of nightmare hits. When those take off, I'll add LinkedIn and YouTube, but this will do for now. There's a method to my madness, just like the dreams it inspires."

Cassandra peered through the glasses. "I don't see the subliminal."

Shannon shook his head. "Same here."

Pedro adjusted the image. This time, the words appeared. *I am your whole truth. A vote for me is a vote for you.*

The wave of text moved as fluidly as the image, barely noticeable unless you stared long enough. It was dizzying, like watching words float in and out of reality.

"Okay, not there without the glasses." Shannon took his glasses off, squinting at the wall. "Can the average person see it?"

"It's not the subliminal message with your eyes open that matters, sir," Pedro explained wearily. "The key here is the dreams. The real magic is in the subconscious, what happens when people close their eyes. I've coded it so that most people who see this image will dream of you, whether they want to or not. And even if they don't dream about you, they'll be curious about what it must be like to meet you in their dreams, because everyone else is. FOMO will set an unconscious intention to dream of you. Either way, images of you are running inside their heads 24/7. That kind of relentless influence wins elections — and just about everything else."

"Hmm." Shannon sounded unconvinced. "I'm more inclined to be sold on the subliminal message you encoded in my image. Tell me, how did you do it? And can you teach others how to do it? What's your price for that nightmare code?"

"All the information is stored in encoded files on my computer and iPad. You *could* get a team of tech geeks to hack into them and learn how to do a basic limited campaign. But for the kind of campaign that can create a real shift, they will be missing one crucial secret ingredient, and that bigger campaign won't be a success without it."

"And what's that?"

"With all due respect, Mr. President, if I told you, it wouldn't be a secret. And it would also completely reduce my worth. I will give you a clue: the missing code that makes this dream campaign come alive is not recorded anywhere." Pedro tapped his head. "No backup. It's hidden only in my memory, and that's where it will stay."

Juliana came back in, carrying a strange device that looked like a child's periscope.

"I know I wasn't officially invited," she said. "Pedro is right, the dreams are powerful. But this is what kids are using these days to 'see auras' and I thought it might be useful. They point it at someone, and it supposedly reveals their true nature."

"How?"

"It reveals the person's chakra, or invisible energy surrounding them. Colors, emotions, everything."

"You're kidding, right?" Pedro smirked.

"No. It works." She passed him the periscope. "Just point it at someone and look."

Pedro played along, raising the periscope to his eye and aiming it at Shannon. The result was jarring: a violent red explosion, dark swirls—burning fury coursing through him.

Next, Cassandra. A deep, suffocating blackness covered her entire form. Her sister was different: soft pink.

Finally, Newman. The colors around him were faded, like a check shirt that had been through too many washes.

"Well?" Juliana asked.

"I'm sure this would prove useful for law enforcement and relationship issues."

The President brushed past Pedro's sarcasm. "Thank you, Juliana. If I say this periscope has the power to tell the truth, it has power. People are gullible. They're easily swayed by whatever narrative is being spun now. Control the algorithms, create the truth. Get inside them, get their attention and their votes will follow. I want you to make them see shooting stars when they point this thing at me."

"Not my area of expertise. I'm your big-dream guy, remember, not your kaleidoscope guy?"

"Periscope," corrected Juliana.

This toy might be a good distraction for the President, Pedro thought, an escape route for Pedro if things went south. "But I'll give it a go."

"Don't forget, you're on our radar," Cassandra said to Pedro as she started to escort the grinning President out.

"Then you already know I'm flying to the U.K. tomorrow for a book signing. Best I get out of the U.S. when this campaign launches. I'm sure your eyes will be following me, but you really have no need to worry. Did you know a growing number of people there are dreaming about Alice too?" He ignored the face she made. "While I'm there I'll do some research on the impact of dream hacking outside the U.S. If Alice's dreams are filtering out, Shannon's won't be far behind. Everything about his campaign is bigger and better. Soon everyone will be dreaming about President Shannon. I can promise you that."

Pedro pointed the periscope he'd bought immediately on leaving them—which proved addictive—through the window at his wife. Leah sat slumped in a chair on the front porch in the morning sun. She looked lost in her thoughts, as if something was weighing on her.

Her image flickered into focus: above her crown or top of her head chakra, the color was yellow. Was it physical? Emotional? Or something darker? He moved lower to her forehead: a violet pulse of light. Her throat chakra: a blazing, fiery red. What the hell was happening to her?

He stepped outside, the air smelling faintly of earth and rain. The scent unsettled him, as though the world was about to shift on its axis. Leaning down, he kissed the top of Leah's head, imagining his lips brushing against the dense, polluted yellow that clung to her.

"Ever seen one of these?" He held out the toy.

"A periscope? Sure. Had one as a kid." Her gaze flicked to the device in his hand. "But I've never seen one called *I SEE WHO U R*."

"I hadn't either. Look through it and turn it on me. Tell me what you see."

"Okay. Is this like a game?"

"I think it's something more intense. Probably used in spy work or surveillance."

Leah lifted the periscope to her eye, then dropped it as if it had burned her. "What the hell is this thing?"

"What colors did you see?"

"It was like a fire. Raging around you. Interspersed with black holes." She saw his face. "Pedro, you look scared. Like, really scared."

"Just thinking about the U.K. and my talk. It's a big deal. And I'm a nervous flyer."

"You'll do great. You always do. Your fans will swarm around you. I'll be there cheering you on, and your mother too. Team Pedro. Hope it's not all work, work, work, though—we need some quality time together. I have a lot I need to tell you."

We need to talk always felt like a vague threat. "Can't wait," he said slowly.

Chapter 21

Ward may have been Cassandra's assistant for years, but these days he felt like her puppet—her sycophant, her fucking toady. She was the reason he couldn't look at himself in the mirror. She was the reason he felt stuck.

"What am I supposed to do in the U.K.?" Ward sat with his boss in her Orlando condo's sleek living room. "Why do you want me to shadow Garcia? Send a Secret Service agent. Send—"

"I'm sending you because you've been involved from the start and we don't want other people involved, do we."

Things might've been different if Shannon had been his boss, Ward thought. If he'd been the President's communications adviser, he would've pushed for transparency, honesty—a break from the constant cycle of lies, threats, and hyperbole. The world was getting fed up with spin, with alternative facts, with screaming and attention-seeking online.

There had been whispers, of course, stories behind Cassandra's back: rumors of her affair with Shannon and her growing influence over him. Few people in the Administration liked her. But Cassandra didn't care about any of that, unless it threatened her job. If she had the President's favor, she was untouchable, or so she thought. Only now, as the public's opinions shifted from her boss, was she starting to pay attention to what they thought about him. But not about her. Never about her.

Outside her window, a sprawling lake shimmered in the sunlight as if diamonds were scattered across its surface. There were myriad lakes in the city, but this view always caught Ward. It felt magical, almost alive. Like the light was playing a haunting melody on the water. Could anyone else hear it? Was there a twin soul out there who also longed to hear it?

"Suppose I don't want to go?"

Cassandra interlaced her fingers. "So, you're resigning?"

He stared out at the lake.

"Good. Worry about your conscience when all this is over. I just need to know Garcia isn't selling us out to anyone. Whether that's enemies inside or outside of this country, or someone double-dealing behind our backs."

"Like whom exactly?"

She waved a hand. "The opposition. The FBI. The richest people on the planet. Or pick a country. Russia. North Korea. China. Iran. Iraq. United Kingdom. Europe. Iceland..."

"I am not a trained spy. How am I supposed to figure that out?"

"You are not a spy, but you are clever. Use your smarts. Start with his phone. His computer. His devices. Do everything you can, get him drunk I don't care, just try to get hold of his dream hacking formula."

Ward despised himself for how much he liked her flattery. "When does he leave for the U.K.?"

"He's already on his way. We suspect he's going to stay with his mother, so we've booked you on a private flight and into a hotel nearby. You'll have a diplomatic passport—extra immunity if anything goes sideways."

"Like what? I get caught stealing his phone. Pocketing his iPad?"

"I suspect—hope—you're better at this than that. Just don't get caught. I won't be there to save you." Cassandra went in for the kill. "You can track your beloved Alice too and keep her safe."

"She's not my beloved. Anyway, she won't be there."

"Do you think I'm stupid? I told you; I'm a human lie detector. It's obvious to me you've got a bit of a thing for her. Whatever. And she will be there. The CIA, in its infinite stupidity, thinks that sending her and her half-wit team to his talk will somehow throw him off his game, and he'll slip up and spill something he knows. More likely she'll end up hurt. Which gives you a chance to be Captain America and save her from herself. Just make sure you don't let Garcia out of your sight. And if he starts to spill any secrets to anyone, do what you can to silence him."

"But Garcia knows me."

"We thought about that. If he knows he's being watched, there's no way he'll be spilling the beans. Which is why we've got other plans. Nancy? You can come in now."

A woman stepped into the room, wearing a soft green top and leggings, her skin so flawless it looked airbrushed. Even casually dressed, everything about her seemed elegant.

"Thanks for coming, Nance," Cassandra said.

"So good to see you, girl." They shared a fist bump. Then Nancy turned to Ward. "Well now. You are my makeover?"

Cassandra said, "Yes. What do you think?"

Nancy scanned Newman from top to toe. "Not a walk in the park, but I can change his appearance. His features aren't defining. Not an issue. I'll work my magic."

"Nancy is a makeup artist and costume designer," Cassandra told Ward. "She works off Broadway when she's not working for us."

Nancy turned his face left and right, her hands light but thorough, studying him. "Ever had a beard and moustache?"

"Nope."

"Beard, moustache... change your hair. Your own mother won't recognize you when I'm done."

She covered him in a light robe, laying out her tools and getting to work.

The clock ticked away. At last Nancy handed Ward a small mirror. His eyes were now a bright unnatural shade of green; his hair lightened to a white hue. A thick, dark beard and moustache were startling against his pale skin.

"Now the hair," Nancy blow-dried and teased it into a windblown allure. She stepped back and surveyed her work. "What do you think of the new you?"

A stranger stared back at him: polished, dangerous—someone you wouldn't want to make an enemy of. "You're right about one thing. I'd be unrecognizable to my mother."

"And to Cassandra," Nancy said. "I'll text her to come back in."

Cassandra froze at the sight of him. "Goddamn. You look incredible. Nice work, Nance. I almost fancy him myself."

"I've trained him how to maintain," Nancy gave Ward a bag filled with spare moustaches and beards. "You'll need these. And I'd urgently recommend different clothes. Something... sharper."

"What, no jeans?"

"Jeans are fine if they are designer jeans, which your current ones certainly aren't. But you'll want dressier shirts. Sweaters that look like they cost more than your monthly paycheck. And ditch those ghastly sneakers, please." She eyed his worn running shoes. "Boots. Something comfortable, but with class. You'll be walking a lot more than you are used to in London. Walking in the footsteps of ancient history over there."

Ward had never visited the U.K. Except in his mind, watching *James Bond* movies.

"Loving this new you," Cassandra startled him by saying. "Not sure I want you to switch back when this is all over." She led Nancy out. "I have fond memories of London. I almost wish I was going with you. Except you won't have time for sightseeing." She gave Ward a hard look. "I need your eyes trained 24/7 on Garcia."

Part Three

Nightmare

Humans are on the whole less good than they imagine themselves to be. To paraphrase Carl Jung, everyone has a "shadow" aspect to their personality, which consists of repressed or unwanted parts of themselves. And the more someone denies or ignores this shadow, the more powerful and potentially destructive it can become.

Part Three

Nightmare

Chapter 22

Pedro Garcia had always loved Soho. It was in his blood — the pulse of London, throbbing with music, art, and culture. The streets buzzed with purpose; the strains of Beatles music drifted from an open window as he and Leah walked.

They meandered toward Covent Garden, dodging tourists and posing for selfies next to the fountains and statues of Trafalgar Square. Pigeons scattered at their feet. Every time a red double-decker bus rumbled past — every few seconds, it seemed — Leah would squeal, like a child spotting a toy.

Stopping at Covent Garden, they got caught in the hypnotic rhythm of talented street entertainers. The atmosphere sweetened as they made their way down a winding Leicester Square backstreet toward Raven Occult Books, tucked away amidst glossy art galleries and high-end designer stores. The air was thick with the scent of fresh pastries from cafés whose croissants were so flaky they almost collapsed under their own weight.

"Shouldn't we be having a proper cream tea? This is London, after all," Leah said. "And I've always wanted to see King's Cross and find Platform 9¾. Ever since I read the Harry Potter books. Let's head there."

"I only read the first one… watched the movies with you. J.K. Rowling's a billionaire now, though. And let's save King's Cross for another day. I need to visit Raven before tonight to check everything's set up just right."

Leah was determined. "Cream tea, then."

They sat at a wobbly table, the classic tourist trap of London's old cafés. Pedro was explaining that there was actually no 9¾ platform when Leah unexpectedly announced, "Pedro, I've been married to you for two decades. These online dream stories have your brilliance sprinkled all over them — you've got to be involved in some way."

"Top secret. NDAs." Pedro couldn't help himself, "But let's say I am one of the consultants on the Shannon re-election team."

"I knew it! So proud of you. You helped create this 'strong man of the people' image, and yesterday, after I saw it on Instagram and took a little nap, bingo—there he was, yelling at me in my sleep. It was a little intimidating in the dream, but when I woke up, I felt so honoured he chose my dreams to appear in."

Pedro couldn't bring himself to tell her she hadn't been chosen.

"I bet there's a subliminal message in there," she said, "something like, 'Hey, I'm one of you, vote for me,' right? Or maybe something for the Latino voters? 'Amigos, soy tu amigo.'" Her accent was atrocious. "Would you like me to help your team create a Spanish version while you head over to Raven? I'll be in your way there anyway. I can stay here with my scones. Mock up some posts in Spanish."

Pedro already had multiple translation options to roll out, but it had been a long time since his wife had amused him, and she was doing so now. Even with Raven just a few steps away, there was no denying his visit would be easier without her beside him babbling on. "You can create posts in Spanish on my iPad," he told Leah, "or just chill and scone yourself out. I'll be back in half an hour."

The moment Pedro stepped into Raven Books, he felt in his element. The place was a paradox—narrow and cramped on the outside, but vast within. An uneven set of stairs led to the second floor, where a member of staff was on a sliding ladder. Ahead, Pedro spotted a big table stacked with copies of his books, chairs arranged in neat rows in front of them. All the greats had spoken here—Eckhart Tolle, Deepak Chopra—names that rang with authority. Now Pedro Garcia would be one of them.

NEW YORK TIMES BESTSELLING AUTHOR, PEDRO GARCIA WILL BE HERE TONIGHT FROM 7–8 PM TO TALK ABOUT HIS BOOKS AND YOUR DREAMS. JOIN US!

A poster showed a pensive Pedro from his first author photograph, taken 15 years ago. He hadn't changed a bit.

He walked over, letting his fingers trail across the spines of his books. *Your Dream Archetype Shapes Your Story: What's Yours?* published five years ago, was on top. He'd never loved the title, but the editor had insisted, and she'd been right. It had made him a fortune, hitting the *New York Times* bestseller list for months, and going into a third printing. Surrounding *Your Archetype* were his first two bestselling books, *Dreams Alive* and *The Big Dream Game*.

His most recent release, *The Rogue Archetype: We All Have This One*, had already outsold its predecessor. It had earned him a substantial raise at the University of Florida, not to mention more sabbaticals than he knew what to do with, and a kind of rock-star status among his students. Even if his theories never received the academic endorsements they deserved from his peers.

"Pedro, so good to see you!"

He caught a whiff of marijuana before he looked up to see Raven's owner smiling almost reverently.

"Claire!"

Claire Easton was a proud Wiccan in her early 50s. She wore her faith like a badge. The lace of her top matching the gothic atmosphere of the store; black eyeliner smudged slightly under her eyes.

"We've got stacks of people signed up." Clutching her pentagram-shaped necklace, she lowered her voice. "Strictly between you and me, more than Tolle's last visit."

One of the oldest esoteric bookshops in the world, the store had been founded during the height of the spiritualist era; allegedly it had been haunted by psychic researcher and Sherlock Holmes creator Arthur Conan Doyle. Raven had been in the Easton family for over a century. Claire had inherited it from her parents. Over the last decade, with the rising interest in the paranormal and conspiracy theories, it had grown exponentially, becoming the go-to place for anything related to the emerging science of consciousness.

When Pedro was younger, his mother and father had made a big deal of taking him here. Pedro had spent hours in the second-hand section, flicking through dusty old books that reeked of age and secrets. One had even become his mantra: Norman Vincent Peale's *The Power of Positive Thinking*.

"Think you can, and you will," his father said. Back then, it had felt like real magic: if he dreamed it, he could do it.

Now he was living it. And he was luxuriating in the one thing his parents had never had: money.

"What are you going to talk about?" Claire asked.

"The rogue archetype, of course. What's yours?"

"My rogue sells subversive books to unlock minds. What about you?"

He'd spent countless hours reflecting on that very question. "Manipulator of beliefs."

"Well, that's not in your book, is it?"

"For good reason." He tapped his nose and whispered, "Just between us."

"Well, I've got some competition for you. I dreamed about this Alice woman. The media's calling her 'the Night Born' now. Guess it won't be long before she sells out and writes her story. Have you heard of her? She's a dream expert. Not a major one like you—though after all this, who knows?"

"I know about the 'dream made me do it' murder case. What was she doing in your dream?"

Claire traced the cover of *The Rogue Archetype*. "She was showing me this."

That something he'd created was taking on a life of its own gave Pedro an eerie feeling. "What did she say to you?"

Claire said, "She handed me your book and said, 'Read it.'"

"Anything else—anything terrifying?"

"Nope. It was a happy dream. I woke up feeling so energetic afterwards. And when I woke up, my copy of *Rogue* had been delivered through my letterbox! And now I'm speaking to you. Synchronicity, right? Foreshadowing."

The dream itself is synchronicity. Was his Alice campaign getting weaker? Nightmares were now transforming into visions.

He changed the subject. "How many signed up for tomorrow?"

"Two hundred and forty-two so far, and we have barely advertised. We'll be packed. It's going to be brilliant."

He eyed the space. "Do you have room for that many?"

"I'm planning to set up 100 chairs, but we can squeeze a few more in, and the rest can stand. If it gets too crowded, people can sit in the café or wander around. You'll have a mic, so they can hear from anywhere."

Raven Books felt like a refuge now, a place where he could retreat and live his big author dream one more time before letting it go and stepping into the bigger dream game. He thought of Leah waiting patiently in the café; she hadn't responded to his texts urging her to come to the store. It wasn't like her. But she had looked so at ease. And she knew where he was; she could always head over if she got bored.

"This way," Claire led him toward the bookshop café.

Her words about synchronicity pricked at him. Or was there something far deeper at play? He'd find out tonight.

Retracing his steps to the bakery, he pushed open the door. The wobbly table where Leah had been sitting was now occupied by a young couple struggling to keep it steady. Pedro approached them. "Did you happen to see a woman here working on an iPad?"

The man barely looked up. "Maybe ask the server."

Pedro made his way to the counter, toward a young man with a name tag.

"Can I help you, sir?"

"My wife was sitting at that table. She was working on an iPad. Now she's gone. Did she leave anything behind?"

The server shrugged. "She left about an hour ago. Ah, yes, she asked me to give you this note."

I've got one of my migraines, my love. It's foul. I need to find somewhere quiet to sleep it off. Sorry I'll miss your talk—you'll be astonishing as always. Enjoy. See you afterward at your mom's; I'm heading there now to grab some pills and sit in a dark room. Sorry I didn't text earlier—my phone died. Call your mom.

He dialled his mother, who was already on her way to Covent Garden. She was bringing two of her friends along to Pedro's talk, after they had a quick bite. "Don't worry, Leah's back at mine, love, safe and sound in Battersea." She went on about how tired Leah looked, how many aspirins she had given her, and how Leah had been snoring when she locked the door and left.

"Did she bring the iPad?"

"It's on the kitchen table, charging. Do you need it for your talk? I could head back to get it for you."

It was better that the iPad was safe in Battersea rather than with him at the store. "No, don't worry. I'll see you there." He would treat himself to a light supper somewhere outrageously expensive and prepare for his presentation. Leah would be fine waiting for him, resting in peace and quiet. She always was fine with everything. It was her chosen role in his life: to be whoever he wanted her to be.

Ward trailed Garcia and his wife as they meandered through the central London crowds for hours. When they entered a bakery, he settled at the table behind them. At one point, Garcia had turned and looked him directly in the eye as he moved his chair, but Ward saw no sign of recognition.

He was in disguise—a new man. Nancy's handiwork had been impeccable. He'd checked himself in the airport restroom that morning after he'd gotten off the plane, giving his beard and hair the right amount of unruly. Newman BT (before transformation) felt like a distant memory. He had become Newman 2.0, AT.

As he tackled his first cream tea, he listened to Garcia and his wife talk about Harry Potter. By his second scone, Ward was losing his battle against sleep and jet lag. He rested his head on his arms. Within moments, reality faded away.

With Alice's face came the strains of classical piano music, a familiar melody. The terror of their previous dream meetings was gone; Ward felt a powerful love; everything seemed beautiful, meaningful. Alice opened her mouth, but no words came out. He tried to speak, and the same thing happened. But they were talking with their feelings.

"Sure, sure," a man's voice broke through. Ward's eyes opened. Garcia was standing before Leah. "I'll be back in 30 minutes, tops."

As Garcia slipped out of the café, Ward put a £20 note on the table, grabbed his things, and followed, until he saw Garcia enter Raven Bookshop: The Store of Never More.

Chapter 23

The flight stretched on and on. They'd been airborne for hours.

Joe slipped out of his seat and made his way over to Alice.

"Joe," she whispered into the dark. "It's lights out and sleep. Why are you still wearing jeans?"

"Remember *Lost*?"

"You think we're going to crash on an island?"

"It's just a self-comforting thing."

"I'm glad I'm not the only one who feels like an imposter. I keep expecting someone to pop out and say, 'Smile, you're on camera.'"

The plane hurtled forward through the night sky. Sleep eluded Alice for what seemed like an eternity. Then her breath slowed: she found herself in the middle of a dream.

A lucid dream: she knew she was asleep and dreaming. Unless she was dead and wandering the afterlife. But she didn't feel dead.

This place—this world—was a labyrinth of shifting shadows and muted tones, punctuated by the occasional burst of color that seemed out of place, like neon graffiti on a crumbling wall. The atmosphere was crisp, almost sweet, reminiscent of spring, fresh and alive. Alice wandered deeper, unsure where she was going.

Then, in a blur of shifting fog, she saw Ward Newman smiling and waving goodbye. A woman who looked exactly like Alice was walking toward her. Even their eyes mirrored each other—the crystalline blue, the deep, warm brown. The woman seemed to have materialized from the air and now walked in step beside Alice. Her presence felt magnetic, unsettling.

Her surroundings were unfamiliar, but soon she recognized the cabin's faintly rustic décor. She wasn't dead, she was on a plane, heading somewhere fast.

People often met departed loved ones in dreams, an experience that was comforting and meaningful. But this wasn't a meeting with a departed soul. It was a confrontation, a merging of worlds, an encounter with something, someone spiritual, that felt like it had always existed within her. It was her. Had she met her future or her higher or her afterlife self?

She needed to write it down. She had to remember her dream—her vision—so she could relive it whenever she felt incomplete.

Alice snatched her red journal from the plane's seat pocket, scribbling furiously. It had been months since she'd researched so called afterlife dreams.

She had always been skeptical about the possibility of a spirit world. The stories of people's transformative near-death experiences—seeing a light, hearing voices, feeling a presence not physical but undeniably real—fascinated her. She couldn't quite commit to belief, though.

Could consciousness survive death? Maybe it was possible. After all, everything was energy, wasn't it? Thoughts, emotions, memories couldn't just vanish when a body died. Energy never died. It just transformed.

I will not submit to the fashionable stupidity of dismissing everything I do not understand as fraud; she recalled Jung's words. This vision, this encounter, wasn't fake. It had felt more real than anything in her life. Something to ponder more deeply when all this craziness was over.

She turned toward the window and yanked the shade open. The first light of dawn was creeping across the horizon, transforming the sky in gold and rose. This was it. The secret she had been handed; if she believed in her future or her higher self, she could make a difference. Do some good in the world.

Could she succeed where others had failed? For centuries mystics, healers, even hopeful skeptics like Alice, had tried to change the world. Could she wield her hidden powers to make the impossible real?

"Of course we can," Joe read her mind.

"How?"

"Follow our lead. We'll take care of you."

Alice turned away; it was the worst possible thing he could have said. This was no dream. It was her mission, her higher calling, the stuff dreams—and reality—were made on.

And she wasn't about to follow anyone.

The Grangers fought off yawns, faces sagging with exhaustion, as they landed in Gatwick. Joe looked ready to collapse. Alice was almost sleepwalking. Matt and Chico lagged, watching Griffin step up to the immigration desk.

She handed over their passports. Her agency I.D. seemed to help; they breezed through customs.

At the arrivals gate, Alice's mother stood in the small crowd, waving enthusiastically. They hadn't seen each other in what felt like forever. Willow Sinclair stood a little over 5 feet 10; her dancing brown eyes gleamed with warmth. Her silver hair was cut to perfection, framing her high cheekbones. She opened her arms wide as Alice hurried toward her.

Stepping from the embrace, she ran her fingers through her daughter's dyed hair. "Your disguise works a treat. I only recognized you because you said you'd be traveling with a small group. And, of course, Luna."

As if on cue, the dog trotted up. Willow bent down to her. "My favorite pooch in the world." Luna smothered her in slobbery kisses before Alice took her leash.

"Come on, Mum. Let me introduce you to everyone."

The group was waiting outside when they reached the terminal doors, shielded under the terminal's awning. A procession of cars, taxis, and minibuses lined the curb, their engines idling in the cool morning air.

"This is my mum, Willow Sinclair," Alice announced with pride. They all introduced themselves.

"I've got a van waiting," Griffin was brisk. "You'll all fit, and there's plenty of room at your safe house in Kensington."

Barnes said, "I'll cook for everyone. We can catch up, get everyone up to speed."

"That is very kind, but I'm the cook here, Mr. Granger," Willow exclaimed. She hooked her arm through Alice's as they walked toward the van.

The familiar scents of green parks and fields mingled with the undertones of city dust, petrol fumes, and something distinctly exotic. The air smelled different here compared with Florida. Alice was still weary after the long flight, but something about the crisp atmosphere woke her up.

The drive to Kensington was surprisingly quick; the normally congested roads were clear, as if the universe had decided to speed them along, red lights turning green in perfect harmony. Griffin parked in front of a charming two-story house off a quaint, narrow street of old buildings and cobbled walkways, quintessentially British. Alice let the beauty of it all sink in—the symmetry of the buildings, the history etched in every stone. London seemed like a postcard come to life.

Nothing like this existed back home in Florida. Aside from St. Augustine, which for all its history was a mere infant compared with London's grand two millennia, Florida was mostly swamps and beaches, the land shaped by nature's indifferent hand. London, on the other hand, stood as a living monument to centuries of bloodshed, power, and reinvention.

Luna pulled at her leash toward a tiny park nearby. Alice let the dog lead her into a patch of grass. The scent of the earth was different here, rich with age. Luna bounded around, heedless of the ancient history surrounding her.

According to the Gregorian calendar, London had been founded in 43 CE when the Romans, led by the notoriously cruel Emperor Claudius, had first set foot in Britain. It was hard to imagine when she read about it in grad school that this very green and pleasant land of Shakespeare, who famously coined the 'stuff that dreams are made on,' as well as the visionary minds of Austen, Dickens, and her beloved Tolkien, had once been ruled by emperors and gladiators. An ancient world, all testosterone and bloodshed, with women often little more than an afterthought—a footnote to the wars of men.

That viral image of her was like a modern-day Colosseum. A digital arena where the stakes were as high as any life-or-death contest in ancient Rome.

But Alice wasn't about to die in some grand spectacle like those gladiators. This time, the fight would be on her terms.

A few hours later, when they had all settled in, Alice paced, looking at her watch and thinking about her father. She was more than ready to meet him—but on her own terms. She needed to act, not just follow orders.

She could take the initiative and talk to the press.

There was a London-based journalist who had reached out to Alice in America. He'd been one of the few journalists to see her as a human being and more than just a viral sensation. She couldn't forget his name: John Bond.

Going through her email, she found his thread.

You're probably feeling overwhelmed, the most recent one said, *maybe even wanting to disappear, but I would really love to interview you.*

He worked for several major news outlets. Maybe he could be the key.

John, it's Alice Sinclair, she texted him. *I'm in London. I've got a story for you. Can we meet? Where are you?*

As if daring herself, she dropped her address in the message, sent and immediately deleted it.

OMG, I can be there in less than 5. Will meet u out front.

I'll be sitting on the steps with my dog.

Wow! Last night I dreamed about u, Alice, and in the dream, you were tossing me balls and Frisbees as if I was your dog. Already on my way.

Waiting on the porch steps with Luna, Alice zipped up her jacket in the crisp air.

A man was jogging down the pavement, his shoes tapping out a rhythm in the quiet of the neighborhood. As he neared, he lifted his hand to wave. Alice waved back.

Breathless, he reached them, dropping onto the step next to her. "Blimey. This is bloody brilliant."

"This is…"

John Bond had a rugged real-world appeal—sharp jawline, piercing blue eyes.

"May I record this interview?" He held his phone as if it were an extension of his hand.

"Absolutely."

As Alice shared edited highlights of the strange journey that had brought her here, Luna sprawled out on the pavement, glancing between them.

Alice couldn't help asking him about his name.

"No relation, sadly. My old man's surname was Bond, and he and my mum were both massive James Bond fans. They thought *John* would work. Didn't quite think it through. But it's become my signature now. My writer's calling card."

"I've read your articles on *Reality Check*. I love your work. You don't take sides; you just report the facts. You may be the last natural-born journalist to do that."

"And this could be my biggest scoop yet. Election interference, deep-state mind control, the whole bloody thing. I could have it on *The Reality Check* site by morning. After that, if you're still okay with it, I'll bleed it out to other major media outlets."

"Perfect. And swing by Raven Books tonight. Pedro Garcia's talking there, and things might get real interesting. I'm planning something that should startle him, maybe get him to reveal some major dish."

"Count me in."

"Where have you been?" Back in the house, everyone swamped Alice. "Sit down. You've got to hear this."

"I had Chico track Garcia and his wife ahead of his talk," Griffin told Alice. When Garica left Leah alone in a tearoom, Chico had taken a leap of faith and approached her. He'd shown her his CIA badge.

"We believe your husband is involved in election subversion," he'd told her.

Leah hadn't needed any encouragement to hand over the iPad and become the hero of the midnight hour. It felt heaven sent. She'd been looking for a way out of her marriage for the last few years. She was in love with another woman, her personal trainer, but couldn't leave Garcia as she had not signed a prenup. Handing over the iPad was her ticket to emotional and financial freedom from a loveless marriage. Chico was waiting outside Garcia's mother's flat. Once she left to attend her son's presentation in Soho, Chico would enter and escort Leah and Garcia's iPad to a private U.S. bound flight.

"The coding is in the iPad?" Alice said. "We've done it, then! We've won."

"Yes and no. We don't know what our tech team will be able to decode. The more evidence we can get, the better. Right now, he doesn't know his wife has flipped, but time isn't on our side. We need to get under his skin, but not too much." Garcia had dual citizenship, which meant he might find a way to escape and claim immunity in the U.K.

"Maybe we should just freak him out so much with our fandom and tireless questions about the Alice dream image he flies home right away to get away from us."

What would his fans think of the spiritual guru when they stood up in the middle of his presentation and made their identities known? How would his adoring followers react?

Alice checked her watch: 5:55. Her sketchy but intuitive knowledge of numerology kicked in. The number 5 meant change. Break everything down to build it back up again. Was this an invitation for chaos to reign, or a brave new future to be built?

Luna padded into the kitchen and sat in front of Alice, gazing up at her.

Alice hugged her. "Sorry, girl. You're staying here." She wanted the dog by her side at the pivotal moment of seeing her father for the first time. But her gut told her Luna should stay exactly where she was.

When you couldn't predict the future or trust your dreams, all you could do was listen to your gut.

Chapter 24

An hour before the event, Ward was back at Raven Books. Earlier that day he'd shadowed Pedro there. He liked the feel of the space. All the books seemed to beckon to him. What was stopping him from reading and dreaming there with his eyes open along with everyone else in the world? He could discover more about himself, about what life was meant to be.

He moved among the stacks, sampling books he wanted to read.

There was a giant poster on the wall promoting that night's workshop: *Unlocking the Unconscious Mind with the Help of Your Rogue Archetype: A New Era in Psychoanalysis.*

A polished podium sat front and center, a pile of Garcia's books set up on a table and spilling over into the café corner in anticipation of a crowd. The scent of herbal tea and incense filled the air.

If only it were Alice's talk he was going to attend, and not Garcia's.

A woman dressed entirely in black approached him. "Are you here for Garcia's workshop?"

"I am."

She was clearly the owner or staff member. Raven Books had a distinct personality, and she had to be its pulse. "Well, you'd best reserve your seat." A growing crowd filled the store, settling into chairs. "Did you sign up, sir?"

"I didn't realize I needed to."

"It wasn't strictly required, but…" She was just trying to get an accurate headcount and email address, she added, since Pedro was such a draw.

Newman extended his hand. "Tyler Atkins. Big fan of Garcia's work."

"Have you read *Rogue*?"

"Who hasn't? Brilliant piece of work."

"We can barely keep it in stock."

"Let me grab one of these," he picked a random book from the shelf. "And I'll claim my seat. Thanks."

As the woman moved off, he looked at the book he'd picked up: *Memories, Dreams, Reflections.* Jung. Talk about synchronicity!

He moved toward the chairs. At least 30 women—perhaps a dozen men—were already settled, some engaged in quiet conversation, others leafing through the books on display. He found an aisle seat in the fourth row, far enough back to have a good view but not too close to attract attention. For the next 45 minutes, he watched people file in.

None of them were Alice.

Then she was there. Making her way to her seat, she suddenly looked directly at Ward.

He felt a shock: she couldn't know him, not as he was now — but he could not shake the feeling that she saw through his disguise, through to his exposed core.

He moved back, standing out of her range of vision. As the talk was about to begin, Alice craned her neck as if she were searching for someone. For him.

Chapter 25

The other Night Born crew sat spread out amongst the crowd, waiting for the workshop to start: Alice with John Bond, Joe in a row with the Grangers. Alice's mother stood in a corner with Griffin. Matt stood in the back, observing everything, just in case.

Garcia ambled up to the podium, a fashionable 10 minutes late, and fussed over the mic. "Good evening and thank you for being here. I deeply appreciate it." His voice was deep, for effect. "Namaste." He pressed his hands together, bowing slightly.

There he was: the man who had given Alice life. She flashed to a vision of herself standing where he stood now, her first book in her hands, her own crowd's faces expectant and rapt. She felt the gravity of the moment, the weight of standing in her father's footsteps.

"When Claire graciously invited me to Raven to discuss concepts from my best-selling books," Pedro's voice was smooth, "I decided that for you wonderful dreamers here, this time I would focus on something a little different. Get your phones out, go to your note's app, or if you've brought paper and pen, take them out."

He picked up one of his books. "As anyone who's read my previous book knows, and I'm assuming that is most of you here, we all have an archetype. I want you to think about your three best qualities as a person. They can be a word, a phrase, or a sentence." The women and men in the front row hung on his every word, Alice noticed.

What were her three best qualities... *Dreamer, curiosity, finding meaning*. She typed them into the Nighborn group chat:

Griffin: *Take down the fuckers, be true to self, don't give up*

Joe: *Honesty, strive for justice, honour the visions*
Barnes: *Understand the vision, move forward, be intrepid*
Aisling: *Read the vibe, read the person, share*
Matt: *Listen, evaluate, act*

Garcia tapped the mic to get the crowd's attention. "Anyone want to share?" A dozen hands shot up.

Willow was one of them. Alice stared: What if he recognised her? This was a big risk.

"You," Garcia pointed at her. "Fourth row." Willow stood up. "What three traits did you jot down?"

"Remember, forgive, but, if necessary, get even."

Laughter rippled through the crowd. "Interesting," Garcia said. "So, your rogue archetype would be... getting even. An eye for an eye."

"Why do you say that?" Willow asked.

"Because it's your strongest driving force."

"That's not much of an explanation," a voice called out from the back. "Care to explain your rationale?"

"Read the book," Garcia stated. "Anyone else care to share?"

John Bond raised his hand.

"Okay, the man, on the far right, waving your arm like it might disconnect from your shoulder."

"Never give up, search for truth, communication."

"Truth searcher. That's your rogue archetype—the one that makes you stand out."

"Explain, please," John pressed. "And I've already read the book."

"Let's break that down. Someone who searches for truth usually does so at great cost to themselves or others."

"Jung searched his whole life for truth," John continued. "At great expense to others, too. It ruined his friendship with Freud. Probably his marriage as well. But he didn't write about that."

Garcia flustered. "Read *The Red Book* and you'll get it."

"I read it," a woman called out. "Couldn't make sense of it at all. Did you know his family were reluctant to publish it because they thought it might be viewed as evidence of madness?"

Her voice was familiar. Alice strained to see who had spoken. *Amira Mensa.*

What on earth was her friend from campus doing here in London, in this store?

The tension in the room grew palpable.

Garcia tried to regain control. "Okay, let's do yours, youngish lady. What three traits did you jot down?"

"Sir, with all due respect," Amira shot back, "what do you consider *your* three traits?"

Claire Easton stood up in the back. "Excuse me, folks. Pedro Garcia isn't here to talk about his rogue archetype. He's here to generously talk about yours." She spread her arms to include the room. "So, ma'am, perhaps you could answer him. What three traits did you write?"

"What are you," Amira said, "his rogue sidekick?"

People were starting to stand, trying to see what was happening. Taking advantage of the moment's confusion, Alice shuffled over to Amira. "My God, what are you doing here?"

"Friends don't let friends fight all their battles alone. I had to be here; I was there when this all started, remember. I'm not going to let you fall of that cliff I dreamed about." She added, "Griffin kept me up to speed. I'm standing with you. Count me in as an official member of the Night Born."

Garcia was trying to regain control. "The idea with your own rogue archetype, the thing that defines it, is the trait that motivates you to act independently, break from the crowd to shine. Physically, vocally, emotionally, viscerally. It's an immovable force."

Several people raised their hands with questions.

Alice felt a surge of courage and stood up. He immediately pointed at her. "Back row with the multicolored hair?"

"I'm confused. I read your book, and I still don't know my rogue archetype. My three traits are: dreamer, curiosity, finding answers. What does that tell you?"

"Dreamer."

Hearing him say the word that powered her life triggered something in Alice. "Yes, and dreamers tell the whole truth, don't they, Father?"

He stared, starting to speak, but she went on:

"Is the rogue in me the reason you were able to create an image that went viral worldwide? I wonder, did you ever consider the well-being of your daughter, the one you abandoned as soon as you found out she was coming to life? The dreams she had of one day meeting her father? Even my wildest ones couldn't foreshadow something like what you've done."

Pedro's mask slipped as raw panic filled his face. He opened his mouth to speak, but he seemed frozen.

Amira stood up, in solidarity with Alice, as did Willow.

"Yeah," Alice told the crowd, "he did that to me. Look at my face. You might see it in your dreams or nightmares soon. People over in the States are killing each other in my name. And it's a dry run for something bigger. Soon your feeds will be flooded with images of our President. He'll appear in your thoughts, your dreams, your everything. You'll be doing things in his name because a dream made you do it. And the man behind it all, who created this mutilation in our minds is standing right there. You…"

BANG!

A gunshot, followed by another; then the room went dark.

Around Alice, people screamed, knocking over chairs, scrambling to escape. Alice dropped to the floor, crawling toward a column and pressing her back against it. She peered through the darkness for the others in her team.

A man picked up a chair and slammed it through the broken window, escaping through it. Through the stampede of people pushing and shoving, Alice saw Matt move Griffin, Amira, John, and the Grangers toward the exit. Joe was right behind them.

Then Pedro Garcia was lumbering toward Alice, his eyes wide with something she couldn't place. His hand gripped her arm, hard.

The father she had never dreamed of looked twisted with fury. His fingers dug into her skin. "You... you... why?" His voice was venom.

Alice yanked her arm free, adrenaline surging as her elbow snapped upward, driving into his nose.

He staggered back, his hands flying to his face as blood poured from his nostrils. Then he lunged at her again.

Alice felt herself being lifted; someone pulled Garcia away from her. She couldn't help thinking how puny her father looked beside the tall, bearded man who was rescuing her.

It came to her: she knew him. She couldn't explain how, but this stranger she'd never seen before—it was Ward Newman. Then Willow —her *mother*—launched herself at Garcia.

All the fury of a woman who'd spent decades holding back rage exploded. Garcia went down. Willow went down. Newman dived in to separate them.

Garcia managed to get away.

Newman went after him.

Willow's rage was raw; it went through Alice like an electric current.

"That motherfucker," Willow exclaimed. "He got away. He always runs away."

"Mom, the cops are on their way. He won't get far. They'll get him. We need to move."

"I'm here." Amira appeared, breathless. She gripped Alice's shoulder. "You all okay?"

Alice wasn't okay. Not by a long shot.

Chapter 26

"Pedro, just fucking chill!" Ward grabbed Garcia's shoulder, herding him down the sidewalk. "It's me, Newman, I've got you. We need to get out of here."

Garcia was still trying to stem the bleeding. "Take it," Ward shoved a handkerchief into Garcia's trembling hand. They moved fast through the chaos, flashes of lights, screams echoing off the pavement, panicked people spilling from the bookstore.

Finally, they reached a bustling restaurant bar several minutes away from the bookstore. Garcia barged in and immediately headed into the public restrooms there.

Standing outside the restroom entrance like a bodyguard, and ushering away eager waiters wanting to seat him, Ward searched for flights. They had to get away now. Orlando, then maybe Georgia, or California—hell, even Canada, Ward didn't care, as long as he was as far from this bleeding nightmare as possible.

His phone buzzed: Cassandra.

What the hell is going on there? It's filtering into global news. "Workshop at Raven Books by author and global dream expert Pedro Garcia erupted in violence. Four injured, one critical... amid major revelations of dream manipulation."

He opened the clip she'd sent from *The Reality Check*; some journalist who'd been there called John Bond had uploaded a grainy video of the talk and then the carnage inside the store, the aftermath spilling out onto the street. Ward caught a flash of himself, Garcia, and Alice jumbled together.

Shooting twice in the air was the only thing he'd thought to do to stop Garcia from confessing.

We need to get him out of this country, Ward texted Cassandra. *Now. Tonight.*

Let me see what I can arrange. Just get him somewhere safe for now.

Somewhere safe? Where the hell would that be?

Ward banged on the restroom door. "Pedro! Come on, man, open. We need to vanish."

Silence.

He banged again, harder, tried the door handle, slammed his fist against the metal. He needed them both out of here before it was too late.

He barrelled against the door until he broke through, stumbling into the small room. Above the sink the window was open, its glass swinging wide.

The motherfucker.

Pedro wasn't there. Just an open window.

Ward ran out to the street, throwing himself into a cab that came up beside him. "Get me away from here. Now."

"What's going on back there, man?" The driver glanced over his shoulder. "Police, sirens, panicked crowds, ambulances…"

Adrenaline was still coursing through Ward. "It was an author thing. People just… lost it. I don't know what the hell happened."

"People have become kind of nuts these days."

"Yeah." Ward reached for his phone: he had to focus. Find that flight, whatever the cost. Then brace himself to tell Cassandra he'd screwed up: Garcia was on the run.

But it would resolve. In his present state of mind, Garcia would be easy prey.

How had it all gone so horribly wrong? Alice couldn't fathom it.

Broken window glass sprawled across the sidewalk just a few doors down from the bookstore. Blood pooled on the floor, a grim reminder of how quickly things could spiral, with innocents caught in the crossfire. The local police were everywhere, their uniforms like dark shadows against the harsh streetlights.

Griffin and Matt flashed their badges. A police officer pressed them for a statement. "Was this some sort of CIA operation gone wrong?"

"It was supposed to be an ordinary workshop," Griffin shouted. "The author just went berserk. Someone shot out the overhead lights, and people panicked. Maybe the shots came from a deranged fan or someone making some religious protest, given the author was a well-known advocate of hocus-pocus. Look, we're not involved. Our eyes were on him because of the 'dream made me do it' murder case. But nobody's seriously hurt. We just want to leave."

Alice noticed dark purple bruises blooming on her mother's arms, from where she'd thrown herself at Garcia.

"Honestly?" Willow cried. "It felt kind of good to lash out at him. After all these years."

John had taken a video of the whole thing. "*Reality Check* has posted it. It's already going viral. Hundreds of thousands of hits on their channel. Alice, you're a bloody hero."

"The full story isn't out yet," Alice urged. "Knowing a little about dream power can be as dangerous as knowing a lot."

"We're all cleared to leave the U.K.," Griffin broke in. "We head back to the safe house, pack our things. Choppers will be waiting at an airstrip near Chelsea Harbour. Move, everyone. Time is our enemy now. We don't have enough of it."

Chapter 27

Pedro stormed through his mother's Battersea home, yelling, "Leah, pack your things!"

The bedroom felt emptier than usual. Leah was gone; only the faint scent of her perfume lingered.

When he opened the closet, an old T-shirt and a pair of shoes greeted him; everything else had vanished.

She had left him.

He scrambled around the place, searching, but the iPad wasn't here. She had taken it with her.

What was she doing?

He had to find her.

A few years ago, he had suspected Leah was having an affair when she lost a lot of weight, changed her hairstyle and makeup and was barely home, but he had been proven wrong. He'd downloaded a tracking device without her knowledge on her phone, but all it ever showed were routine trips to work, shops, and the gym, so he'd stopped monitoring her, except now and then when it showed the same formula. Leah seemed to live a predictable, unadventurous life.

Checking now, he saw she was heading toward Chelsea Harbour. What the hell was she doing there? Who was with her?

Shoving his things into his bag, he grabbed a knife and charged out toward Chelsea Harbour.

There was a taxi idling by the curb. "Get out," Pedro brandished his knife and jumped into the driver's seat as the man fled. The city passed him by in a blur of neon and shadows, but his mind was clear: *Get to her before she gets away.*

This was going to be the beginning of the real dream game — or Pedro's endgame.

Chapter 28

Alice, Willow, and Joe went to fetch Luna at the safe house, packing up their bags. Griffin and the others were already at the airstrip.

"The chopper should be here in minutes," Griffin told Alice's group when they arrived. "Leah's already airborne with Chico."

Taxi headlights sliced through the darkness. Blinded, Alice couldn't make out the driver speeding directly towards them to wipe them out. But she knew who it was.

"He's here! she screamed.

It was too late.

Matt's first shot rang out. As the bullet hit the taxi's tires, there was a screech, then a hiss of rubber as the vehicle veered to the side, pushing Matt several feet away.

Garcia was already out of the bruised car, a glint of silver flashing in his hand: a knife, jagged and wicked.

Red mist clouded Pedro's vision the instant he saw Alice and her team. Leah had betrayed him, handed over his invention to these people.

The Night Born were his creation. His genius had made them.

The dreams Alice Sinclair was chasing—the power, the knowledge—none of it was hers. They belonged to him.

The world would see that soon enough. They would see his genius, even if it killed him.

And if he was going down, he was going to take them with him.

Matt was navigating around the crashed car toward them when Garcia stormed towards Alice. Willow leapt at him. Savage, he shoved her aside.

Her head hit the gravel with a loud cracking sound. Blood poured out of her head.

Red flooded Alice's vision.

Grabbing the knife as Garcia was getting to his feet, she plunged it into his chest as he lunged like a monster towards her.

Clutching his heart, Garcia toppled over, a look of incredulity on his face.

Alice staggered back. Her hands were bloody as the knife clattered onto the floor.

She rushed to her mother, who was lying with her eyes wide open. Willow gave Alice a long loving look, then closed them.

Joe stumbled to Alice. She clung to him, raw sobs shaking her body. The others crowded around.

Luna's howl pierced the chaos, guttural, haunting.

Alice collapsed. Joe picked her up, her body heavy in his arms.

As Matt lifted Willow's body, they all ran toward the lowered ramp of the waiting chopper.

Once in the air, Joe pulled Alice close, his arm around her shoulders. Luna curled up in the aisle, her watchful eyes never leaving Alice.

Griffin had given her a sedative to calm her, and the chopper was mercifully silent now as they climbed higher, cutting through the night. Joe squeezed his eyes shut and whispered to any spirit that might be listening, *please, keep everyone safe.*

Under the sedative's spell, Alice had a vision behind her eyes.

As if directly from the night an ethereal figure appeared, bathed in a dim, otherworldly glow. Alice pulled Willow to her, desperate to hold on, to feel her mother's presence one more time. Willow soothed Alice's hair, but then pulled back, her gaze locking into Alice's.

Her voice in the dream was tender. "Stop crying and let the world see your eyes, baby. I'm so sorry I ever encouraged you to hide behind those blue lenses, to pretend to be someone you weren't. I'm blessed to have lived long enough to see you reveal your true self. Don't ever shrink yourself to make others feel better. Shine. Shine bright."

Her voice grew softer. "Death ends a life, but it doesn't end a relationship. You know that, deep down. And on the other side? I can do more for you now. I love you, and that never changes. My love is your bodyguard, forever watching over and protecting you. All you have to do is decide what to do with the time that is given to you. Heal your world within. Then go change the world."

Alice woke to a strange sense of peace. In a single night, she had lost both the mother she adored and the father who had intrigued and terrified her, but with the clarity grief brought, the dream had shown her: this was the moment she got busy living, let what no longer served her die.

Something had died: her need to dance to the expectations of a world that didn't truly understand her. No longer would she trust the advice of others over her own intuition.

As dawn broke high in the sky, Alice Sinclair had shined a night-light on her own shadow and was reborn for the first time.

Pedro Garcia could feel his own end nearing. His organs were shutting down, his breaths shallow and labored as the world around him began to blur.

He sensed something—someone—there, surrounding him. Whispering.

He wanted none of them: the ghosts, the voices, the memories. None of the feelings that hovered at the edges of his fading consciousness. He just wanted oblivion. But the feelings closed in tighter, the whispers turning to guttural hums, pressing against his skull, until one thing broke through—

Alice.

She had always been there. Always in his dreams, lurking behind his eyes, always in his body and mind. He just hadn't recalled them.

She was inevitable, the face he'd forced into the nightmares of others. He had sculpted her image in their minds, manipulated them. But he'd never seen her in his own dreams. Not until now.

As his vision drained, Alice appeared. She morphed—into a snake, slithering, coiling around his chest. Then a spider, her legs stretching into the dark corners of his mind, pursuing him, trapping him in a web.

A snake. A spider. Classic dream symbols, symbols of transformation; of things he had always tried to escape from.

The vision of Alice became clearer, more familiar.

The twisted riddle unraveled: she wasn't just some random figure in his delusion. She was his daughter. He felt her pain. He felt Leah's slow burning hatred of him. He felt the pain of everyone he had ever hurt in their dreams.

The woman who had confronted him in that bookstore was part of this unholy equation. The hatred she'd felt—her voice, so full of rage and fire—was cutting through him now.

He hadn't recognized Alice's mother until now. He hadn't recognized Alice. But the connection had been there, lurking, whispering to him all this time.

No, it was just chance. Coincidence. Random, nothing more. Never more. Never more.

The long dark shadow he had cast on the Night Born would remain, even as his blood, his very life force, seeped from him, sinking into the ground beneath him.

His blood. His curse. Let it stain this place, this moment, this final relentless place...

Part Four

Night Vision

Your vision will become clear only when you can look into your own heart. Without, everything seems discordant; only within does it coalesce into unity. Who looks outside dreams, who looks inside awakes. The self is not only the center, but also the whole circumference which embraces both conscious and unconscious.

—Carl Jung

Chapter 29

Dream Maker by John Bond, a **Reality Check** *Exclusive*

Think about it: A psychiatrist creates a viral campaign featuring a woman that he posts on social media, and within days, thousands of people have dreamed about her. Men and women stop her on the street to announce they've dreamed of her, and before long, her freedom is gone, her life turned upside down.

And so begins a story that could be ripped from the pages of a thriller. But the truth beats any fiction a bestselling novelist could dream up. It turns out the whole thing was a test run for a viral program intended to manipulate the unconscious decision-making of voters and in doing so get President Shannon re-elected.

My footage from the bookshop where the truth was exposed can be found on our Reality Check YouTube channel. Click the link here.

Ward put his phone down. Alice had found a way to get her story out, through a major, credible news source. He couldn't help feeling pride at how rapidly she'd done it. Now it was his turn to do something. All he could do was pray that his message would get through to her.

Whether it did or not was entirely outside of his control. For all he knew, the CIA had destroyed her personal phone, which would make her unreachable. All he could do was wait for his life to end—or to begin.

The flight back to Orlando stretched on, endless. Details, past and present, faded from his mind; he felt as if he were in a twilight zone.

Finally, the plane touched down, and the handful of other passengers jumped up, gathering their belongings. Ward sat as if in suspended animation, unable to move. He kept waiting to wake up and find out that everything had been a dream.

It wasn't.

He watched the other passengers exit the plane, seeming so carefree, as if they had all the time in the world.

If Ward survived this, he hoped—desperately hoped—that he'd be able to feel some spark of normalcy, of life. For some reason his mind flashed to the opening and closing scenes of the movie *Love Actually*, a sequence of ordinary but extraordinary expressions of love. But, of course, that was just a slick rom com, no relation to real life. Didn't the British Prime Minister stand up to the bullying of the American President in that movie?

The plane emptied, until Ward was the last passenger to leave. He followed the signs to immigration. Though he kept checking his phone, there was no response from Alice to his text.

His message must not have gotten through. He was a dead man walking. Cassandra was bound to have her team waiting for him, ready to guide him to a parked car with blacked-out windows—perhaps his final destination.

Alice sat in the backseat of a speeding van, staring out into the future, a dark nothingness.

Joe sat beside her, and Luna was watching her on her other side, but she barely felt them. She was numb.

The only sound in the car was the tires humming on the interstate. Griffin gripped the wheel as she drove, her eyes fixed on the road ahead.

All of it had to be a dream, Alice told herself. Her mother hadn't died. Alice scrolled through the albums on her phone, searching for photos of Willow, her sweet mother, as if that would somehow bring her back. Her phone had curated a montage of Alice and her mother into a mini video. A sweeping orchestral score accompanied it. Alice kept playing it over and over.

It had to be a dream.

A text from Ward Newman came through on her phone. Alice stared at his words, unable to think. They floated off into the distance, part of the same dream she was trapped in.

Then the van went over a bump in the road. Alice was jolted back to reality.

She heard herself say, "I just got a text message from Ward Newman that we all need to hear. NOW."

Griffin didn't hesitate and signalled to get off the highway, taking an exit toward a nearby shopping mall. In the parking lot, Alice was on autopilot as she read the message to the others.

"Alice, it's Ward Newman," she read. "I got your number when Cassandra assigned me to track you. She wants me to use her influence to get Garcia's iPad from the CIA and delete all evidence of our meetings. But I'm done. I've got recordings of everything: I had my phone on record all the time, and I'm willing to turn state's evidence. I will be happy to share my recordings with the CIA, the DOJ, the FBI — whoever is going to investigate this mind-hacking scheme.

"Right now, I'm headed back to the U.S. on a private flight that Cassandra arranged for me. She's sending a car to pick me up at Orlando Airport at 8:30 a.m. The flight has sketchy Wi-Fi, so if this message doesn't get through, I am certain she will find a way to silence me — probably threaten my family or crush me in a fatal car accident. If that happens, I want you to know how deeply sorry I am for my part in this, and the fact that you got caught up in it. I pray that truth finds a way."

"Text him back right now," said Griffin. "Tell him help is on the way. The CIA will meet him at the airport and usher him through immigration. We will make sure to put his family in a safe house. Tell him Agent Griffin will contact him on arrival."

Alice was holding her phone, but she seemed unable to find the keys, Griffin saw.

Griffin took it from her and sent the text herself.

Chapter 30

Ward was reading the text from Alice when someone's hand reached out and took his bag. He looked up: it was the CIA agent, Griffin.

"Keep moving. I've got you cleared," she said. "Van at departures. We need to backtrack there, because they'll be waiting for you at arrivals."

Linking her arm through his, she handed him a baseball cap and a long coat, guiding him through the maze of the airport to a small van parked at the curb, tucked into the chaos of airport traffic, where cops waved their whistles and directed the ongoing flow of cars.

Joe opened the van door, and Ward scrambled inside. The door slammed shut behind him.

He was sitting beside Alice, now. But she didn't seem to register that he was there.

From the front seat, her dog, Luna, turned and growled, baring her teeth. She seemed poised to lunge at him but didn't.

Griffin drove out of the airport, her face unreadable. The atmosphere in the van was icy.

"We'll lay low at a safe house," Griffin broke the quiet. "Right now, though, Ward, I urgently need you to transfer all the recordings—everything you have on them—to me."

As soon as she'd given her phone number, Ward started transferring files.

The chill in the car bore down on him. He blurted, "Jesus, Alice, everyone, I'm so sorry. I can't change my past role in all this horror, but I can do everything I can from now on to make this right. This must qualify as election interference, right?"

"It is," Griffin said. "But whether we can pin it on them... We'll see. For now, leave Alice be. Her mother was killed by Garcia last night. She's in shock."

Ward had had no idea. He opened his mouth, but no words came.

Beep. Beep. Beep. The only sound in the car was Griffin's phone as Ward's files came through.

Griffin said, "The DOJ wants to talk to you too. You good with that?"

"Yeah, sure." *I wouldn't call it* good. "Listen, can someone look after my wife? She's expecting."

"We already have your wife, safe and sound. She's being well taken care of. Also, the contact from the DOJ will come to your safe house. He'll take your statement there."

Alice was staring out of the window, as if she didn't register—hadn't even heard—what they were saying. He could feel how numb she was.

If only he could take her grief and pain away. Ward wished with all his heart that he could help bring Alice back to herself. But he couldn't; the burden was hers and hers alone to bear.

Would Alice ever forgive him? Would anyone?

He had no idea what the future held for him. He only hoped that Alice would give him a chance to make amends, let them both start again. That she would let him know her.

But really, none of that mattered. Whatever it would end up costing Ward, he had finally discovered something good and worth fighting for.

"You should go have a rest while you can," Griffin said when they got to the safe house.

Ward had a throbbing headache. When he got to the small bedroom, they'd set up for him, he saw that her team had laid out new clothes for him.

Showering, he changed into a fresh black T-shirt and jeans and lay down, staring at the ceiling. "Jesus Christ." The weight of what had happened pressed down on him.

With any luck, the medication he'd taken would kick in soon. He counted the cracks in the ceiling, waiting for sleep that refused to come.

His phone buzzed. He reached for it and saw a text from Griffin: *DOJ rep is here. 10 min, meet in dining room.*

The ordinary face Ward had spent his life hiding behind was back now. No longer was he inhabiting the persona that Cassandra's stylist had created for him. Gone were the moustache and the beard. He was just the same old Ward, the one he'd been for decades. Combing his fingers through his hair, he started to tuck his T-shirt into his jeans but stopped. *Fuck it.*

He stood in front of the full-length mirror on the bathroom door, tugged his T-shirt free of his jeans, and studied the man who stared back.

How did you go so wrong?

Money. Power. The thrill of being in Cassandra's orbit, the lure of everything that came with being her assistant, her personal lackey. But now who was he? A reviled man, on the run, reduced to begging for mercy from the Department of Justice.

The one power he had left was telling the truth. Providing proof, the evidence that could bring Cassandra, Shannon, and everyone connected to them crashing down.

He studied his T-shirt in the mirror, half expecting to see something bold written across the front. But it was blank. Like him: still a canvas for anyone to project their own meaning onto.

In the dining room, a group had already gathered at the largest table in the room, next to a grand piano by the window. Griffin and Alice, her boyfriend Joe, and several others.

A gray-haired man he didn't recognise sat amongst them. One empty chair waited for Ward.

"This is Max Wild from the Department of Justice," Griffin said. "Come join us."

More introductions were made: the Grangers, Amira, John —
but Ward cut the conversation short. He had an announcement
he couldn't wait a second longer to make.

"The President of the United States, his personal assistant —
Cassandra Mace — and a now-dead psychiatrist named Pedro
Garcia conspired to commit election interference to get Shannon
re-elected. They are still conspiring, because the dream hacking
campaign is still alive in the ether."

Max Wild, the DOJ man, tapped his phone screen. "I recorded
that. Is that okay with you?"

"Why else you think I'm here, Mr. Wild?"

Ward looked over at Alice; she looked so pale and vacant.
"Alice Sinclair was the unsuspecting subject of Garcia's dream-
hacking practice run. But it wasn't about her at all, not really. It
was about creating something — someone — who could become
inevitable."

"That campaign was clever," Wild stated. "I dreamed of
you, Ms. Sinclair, the night after I saw your face online. When
you opened the door earlier, I recalled that dream. You looked
different, but it was you, and you were sitting at a table, talking
with me in a room very similar to this one. You're a psychology
professor, aren't you — can you explain that?"

After a long pause, Alice surprised him by answering.
"Seems like your dream was precognitive. A glimpse of a
possible future."

"You think I'm a psychic?"

Griffin waved her hand, as if to caution him, let Alice be,
but she seemed almost grateful for the distraction and to take
comfort in her dream teacher mode. "In our dreams, we are
all psychic, Mr. Wild. Dreams exist outside time and space.
Past, present, and future happening at the same time. There's
plenty of historical evidence of precognitive dreams. Lincoln
had a dream about his own death. Countless people dreamed
of towers falling the night before 9/11. Dreams can transcend

time. They can reach into a potential future that can play out, as yours clearly did."

Alice said quietly, "I believe your dream showed you a possible future. But what happens next for you depends on the choices you make right now. Right now. You're not bound by your dreams. They are not fate. What matters isn't the dream itself, but how you respond to it. You are not the sum of your dreams. Just like you are not the sum of your thoughts or feelings. You are the sum of your choices."

The room was quiet. Even Luna seemed to be in a reflective mood.

"And that's the problem with Garcia's campaign," Alice implored. "Millions of people could dream of the President and assume he was an inevitable part of themselves and their future. Resistance seemed futile. Then the day after the election, they'd wake up and ask themselves, 'Why on earth did I vote for him?'"

Wild turned to Ward. "How far did Garcia get with his Shannon campaign?"

"Far enough," Ward said grimly. "Almost a hundred million views on Instagram. A couple of hundred thousand filtering into other platforms, but those all came from people sharing and reposting. Garcia hadn't launched it fully on those other sites yet with bespoke posts. What's curious is that the new campaign for Shannon wasn't as polished as the one he did for Alice. He couldn't re-create the same hypnotic magic. That first one was powered by an invisible bond, but the new campaign was only drawing on the power of suggestion. Garcia didn't know that Alice was his daughter."

"Excuse me." Alice pushed back from the table suddenly. "I need to take my dog outside. We need air."

Outside, the late afternoon sun hung low in the sky, casting a golden glow over everything. Luna bounded off to the nearest patch of grass. Birds flew overhead, heading east to the coast or west toward the Everglades, each one knowing its place in the grand design of nature.

But even nature could change. Recently, orcas had been observed hunting great white sharks, behaving in ways no one had expected. Maybe it reflected what was happening here: an aberration of human nature itself—or a brave new world.

An unnatural union between the government and dreams had been unleashed. Things were never going to be the same again. Never again would dreams be dismissed as random.

The nightmares featuring her appeared to be dwindling. Alice was faintly heartened that more and more people, like Wild, were having night visions of her that were precognitive, or healing.

As Alice watched Luna gambol about, the truth hit her again: her mother was dead. Willow, sweet Willow, had sacrificed herself for Alice, knowing the danger. But she had left the invisible force of her unconditional love to forever protect and guide her daughter.

Ward's evidence would seal the deal—it had to. It would be the final piece the DOJ needed to expose everything. And once that all fell into place, Pedro Garcia, her father's carefully orchestrated dream game would fall apart, and the truth would finally be out there.

Wouldn't it?

Chapter 31

His cell phone erupted, vibrating like a trapped fly in a jar. Groggy, Ward fumbled for it, his hand swiping the air, searching blindly in the half-light of his room. Griffin had made him shut it down, but somehow it must have turned itself back on. Or else he had turned it on without knowing he was doing it at some point in the fog of the past days.

His hand found the device at last, answering by muscle memory. There was no caller ID.

"We need to talk."

Cassandra's voice crackled through the speaker, urgent.

Ward's throat was dry. "Nothing to say."

"You're finished. I'll find you, I swear to God, I'll—"

He cut the call.

Years of conditioning to be at her beck and call. How was it possible that he had done this? He should never have answered the phone.

He jumped out of bed and ran through the dark house, sprinting in bare feet toward the kitchen, hallway, living room. Griffin was in the dining room, sitting at her computer, the soft glow of the screen casting her in an eerie light.

"Something's happened," he shouted.

"Ward." She snapped to attention. "Sit down. Talk to me."

He dropped into a chair, letting it all spill out of him— Cassandra's rage, the terrible, creeping certainty that his phone would give their location away. "That call... my phone. It might've led her straight to us."

"Wake up, Ward. I told you to take out the SIM card and turn off the phone entirely." Griffin reached into her bag, then handed him an unmarked phone. "Here. Everything you need is on it—group contacts, all the numbers. Transfer everything you haven't already from your old phone and then destroy it."

His fingers moved almost mechanically as he erased it all: messages, files, photos, texts, contacts. A burst of fury came over him when he had finally finished, he hurled his phone to the floor, stomping and grinding it under his heel. Once. Twice. Four times. The force of his anger completely shattered the plastic, destroying the device.

"Shit happens," Griffin sighed. "It's good you told me. I'll have us all move immediately to another location. Tell everyone to get ready to leave five minutes ago."

"So we're running again."

"Sometimes being on the move is the only option until we figure out the best way forward."

"Look, why don't we confront them? Take every scrap of footage, all the incriminating proof I've shared, and blast it across the media?" Ward pressed. "We need to play their game. Get dirty. If we're going to win, that's how we'll do it."

"Maybe," Griffin seemed unconvinced. "But things need to be thought through. It could create widespread panic and rioting across the nation. Think about it: everyone who has dreamed of Alice and then said or done something they regret because of that nightmare will be looking for compensation. Right now, the priority is to get you and Alice out of here ASAP. You two are the key players. We'll give the others round-the-clock protection."

Before Ward knew it, he was sitting in the backseat of a car. Alice sat beside him; Luna squeezed between them, her head resting on Alice's lap.

"Buckle up," the driver said, and stepped on the gas.

The faint strain of classical music played over the radio, filling the car with a deceptive calm as the driver pushed down hard on the pedal, speeding them away.

"We are on the move because I stupidly answered my phone when I should not have," Ward confessed. "I'm sorry I screwed up—again. Some things never change. I'm deeply, deeply sorry."

Alice was looking out of the window at the tall bamboo and sprawling live oaks native to Florida. Ward was reminded of Tolkien's Ents—those ancient, lumbering guardians of the forest, watching and waiting for something they couldn't quite name.

Alice's voice came, catching him off guard. "Focus on who you are becoming," she said, "not on who you were. Yes, you messed up, but you are human, and humans make mistakes. It's the only way sometimes to learn and grow. It's only through the cracks that the light comes in, or so they say."

She sighed. "Goodness knows I've messed up. I spent my entire life dreaming and not doing. I think that's what connects us somehow. Maybe that's why we see each other in our dreams."

What was she saying? "You've dreamed of me?"

"I didn't recognise at first who I was seeing in my dreams, but it was you."

Alice looked directly at Ward for the first time. He couldn't look away. Time seemed to stop.

"I think we are both works in progress," Alice said. "Others have defined our identity for us—we've let them define us. Because we don't know who we really are, or what we want. At least we realise that now. We've each become aware how much we urgently need to understand and to believe in ourselves. Create our own perspective and reality.

It felt as if she was looking even deeper into him. "Maybe we meet so often in our dreams because we can find loving comfort and completion in each other there. We are so similar. Like looking into a mirror. It's funny, in a way. I used to teach my students about people discovering themselves and who truly mattered to them in their dreams, but I never truly felt it, lived it, until I met you."

"I never truly felt loved in my dreams until you," Ward said. "Is this love?"

Ward noticed the music now playing in the car: it was the very piece that had been playing in his dream-vision in that London café after he'd passed out from too many scones and cream. Joy surged through him.

"Do you know this piece?" Alice was smiling. It's Rachmaninov's Piano Concerto. It was my mother's favorite, from the score for the movie *Brief Encounter*. Two people perfect for each other but meeting at the wrong time. It couldn't be more apt for where we find ourselves right now. You're married—about to become a father, I believe—and I'm... well...

"I'm Alice, only just discovering she has a heart and learning how to use it."

Ward reached out to touch her cheek. She kissed his hand.

"Tell me something." Alice kept his hand in hers. "You worked for Cassandra for three years. You did things for her, things most people wouldn't touch. What changed? What made you stop?"

Ward felt something cave in. "What difference does it make now?"

"It's just my curiosity about human nature," Alice said. "Humans are capable of the most heinous acts: Hitler, Mussolini, Pinochet, Chavez, Maduro, Castro—the list goes on. We can do terrible things to each other. But we can also change. So, what brought you to the truth?"

"Not sure. Something inside me just... stood up for myself."

"Good start. What was the *real* trigger?"

Something had happened to Ward long ago that he had never told a soul. He had always longed to share the memory with someone, but he never had.

He was 6, huddled in his room sorting through his toys, when his mother had stormed in, her eyes dark with fury. Her face was twisted as she spat at him, "Jesus, God, you were the worst decision of my entire life."

Almost immediately his father had rushed in, sweeping Ward into his arms and whispering, "She's lost her mind. I'm taking her to the emergency room, but I'll be back soon."

But Ward's father hadn't come back, not until the next morning. For a long dark night Ward had been left in the big house, alone.

The next day when his father came home, he was alone too. He had committed Ward's mother to the hospital, the first of what would be many stays in a psychiatric facility.

At age 18, Ward ran—he fled his childhood home, his unhinged mother, his passive father. He fought his way through college.

Then, a few years later, his mother killed herself. Ward's father lost himself in a labyrinth of conspiracy theories and falsehoods so deep Ward didn't even recognise him.

Ward had kept the past hidden for so long, even from himself.

He took a breath when Alice said, "Is that it? Childhood trauma? The convenient excuse?"

He stared at her.

"People always blame their parents," she said, "their childhoods. It's too easy. At some point, we all must slash the ties that bind. We must take responsibility for our own decisions. We must grow up. So, go deeper now. What really kept you with Cassandra? And what made you walk away?"

He was ashamed to tell her what he'd realised: proximity to power, the illusion of it was like a drug.

"Eventually, I realized that I was nothing more than her fall guy. I saw how much power corrupts everyone. I thought I could live with it, make them do the right thing. I thought I was making a difference. But in the end, I was blind. Codependent. In love with a lie."

"Your precious. Like the ring of power," Alice said so softly to herself that Ward could not hear her.

"I didn't mean to interrupt you," Alice said, sensing he didn't recognise the reference and had more to share. "Forgive me. Please carry on."

"I had been dreaming of you." Ward continued. "I couldn't stop—I didn't want to stop. But then the dreams of you merged into dreams of Shannon, and he replaced you in my head. I couldn't escape the sight of him. At first, I had these feverish dreams of being buried alive, murdered, executed, or wading through mud, and I was silently screaming, but Shannon just kept watching me, never lifting a finger to help me; it was like he was relishing my desperation. Then I started to have dreams where I was back in school, and Shannon was laughing at me because I'd forgotten the combination to my locker. Or else I turned up to an exam, but I had no idea what the test was about. Or I was in an out-of-control car unable to get to the steering wheel. The whole time Shannon was grinning at me madly, like the Joker.

"I started to wake up wishing I could see you, even if that was a nightmare of you—anything, rather than him, him, him. Then one night I dreamt I saw a baby boy on a river rapid, screaming, waiting for someone to save him, but I couldn't swim fast enough to get there. Then out of nowhere there you were in the river, swimming beside me. *You got this*, you told me. So, I reached out just as the baby was about to fall into a ravine and grabbed him.

"After that, I stopped dreaming about Shannon. And when I stopped dreaming about him, I stopped thinking about him all the time. I stopped wanting to be in his orbit. I wanted to dream a different dream."

"So, in a way, a dream made you do it," Alice observed. "The ability to change our minds when we know better is the source of all hope in this world. And it is the real purpose of dreaming, I think. People like Cassandra always find someone to take the hit for them, a person who believes they're doing the right thing.

"But now the scales have fallen from your eyes. And who knows? perhaps you met your unborn child in your dream or the child in you that you need to put your arms around now and protect and parent with unconditional love. One thing I have learned is that the world is a mysterious place. I think it was Einstein who said that the greatest thing we can experience is the mysterious. But mystery isn't something we *can* experience. Mystery is what defines us. There is so much about our lives, including our dreaming mind, that we need to understand better."

"I wish I could share my dreams with you always." Ward pulled Alice to him, and they kissed. It was passionate, lingering. "And I want you to share yours with me." He started to kiss her again.

But they had arrived at their destination. The meeting of their eyes, minds and hearts a moment now lodged forever, waiting for them both somewhere in time.

Their new safe house was spacious, located in a quiet Windemere neighborhood. It was the perfect cover, though someone with a keen eye might wonder about the security cameras everywhere.

"Where are we at?" Ward asked. "Do you need anything more from me?"

"We're on it," Griffin said.

John Bond and Max Wild were at the house preparing to upload Bond's video everywhere they could.

"How do you think Shannon and the public will react?" Ward asked.

Griffin said, "My guess? He will deny, shift blame, claim he never knew anything about it—blah, blah. Meanwhile, we can't predict how the public will respond: with riots or apathy? Max and I were just discussing it. We want the information out on social media before the DOJ makes their move."

"Why? Can't we do both at once?"

"Because ultimately, it's the people—the voters—who will decide Shannon's fate. They'll either bring him back into office or force him out. And that's where the real power lies. Despite the ease with which those in power believe they can manipulate the public, going so far as digging into their intimate dreams, the real power is still and always will be with the people. And what their collective choice is."

"Not if they've lost their minds," Ward said. "Not if they're being hypnotized. They know not what they do. I'm just praying that when the truth is out there, people will see the light."

Griffin took Ward's hand, her grip strong. "Thank you. People like you—who lose their way and then find their way back—are the only hope we have left. People like you are the game-changers. Since the day Shannon was inaugurated, I've had this gut feeling of repulsion. Now I know why."

She squeezed his shoulder. Patting Luna, she took Alice's arm. "Now, dream team, let's get you oriented."

The house had been repurposed as a fully functioning workroom, rigged up with computers, wall screens, video monitors, and numerous separate stations.

At one of the workstations sat John Bond.

He turned as soon as they came in. "We need to get this material posted now, before they can stop it. It's almost time. We need this out on social media before the White House notices, so it's out of their control. Once they do notice, they will try to shut it down, but the damage will be done by the time the sun comes up. If my faith in human nature and the impulse toward justice holds strong, people will be demanding his resignation by then. And the White House won't be able to bury the truth."

"Interview me," Alice burst out. "I'm a well-known face. I want the world to know the truth from me and to tell my story, uncensored."

John didn't waste a moment before turning the camera on her.

"My name is Alice Sinclair. If you cut me, I bleed; if I sleep, I will dream. If *you* are cut, you bleed; and if you sleep, you will dream. Dreams connect us all as human beings.

"But although we share the ability to dream, the contents of those dreams are sacred—exclusively made for you, and only you, to help you understand yourself and your own inner world better. To help you process and progress from your fears. To help you release mindsets that no longer serve you. Dreams are cathartic. That's why so many of them are nightmares.

"But please don't fear anything your dreams reveal. Take me, for example: in your dreams, I was a nightmare. But the truth is, I'm just Alice. I would never intentionally harm anyone.

"The government, through the unchecked genius of a man named Pedro Garcia, figured out a way to dig deep inside your mind and infect your dreams, permanently traumatizing you with them, implanting fears that are not your own. Like a succubus or incubus, they weren't satisfied with grabbing your attention every moment of your waking day; they wanted—they *want*—to possess you completely, draining the dreams and everything that makes you unique.

"But I must tell you: if you dig deep, even if you see Shannon in a dream, or if I appear again in a nightmare, it doesn't mean you're helpless. You can always take back your dreams, and your own power. You can stop handing it over to others. Your dreams don't happen *to* you. They are created by and for you and are all about you. Believe it or not, you can choose what you dream about and choose how you react to the contents of a disturbing dream. You are always in the driver's seat. Wake up to yourself and your inner power —everyone.

"Whatever you may hear in the coming days, weeks, and months—even if your night visions are filled with terrifying images—your dreams are not evil. They help you face your fears and learn and grow in the process. They offer you an opportunity to transform your pain and trauma into purpose and meaning.

"Your dreams are your sanctuary, your last safe refuge in a world that is battling to take over every aspect of your life. Fight for your right to protect the dazzling uniqueness and infinite creativity of your dreaming mind, and to dream independently. Whatever happens in your lives, don't let anyone ever take away your dreams. They are your best friend, and they tell you the truth.

"And here is my truth, the whole truth and nothing but the truth."

Alice calmly unspooled the story that had begun the day her student Neal King confessed that he had dreamed about her, and others he knew had too. Alice told about the physical and emotional toll it had taken, and how she had discovered to her shock that the man at the center of it, Pedro Garcia, was her father. A man who had abandoned her mother as soon as he learned she was pregnant; a man who had killed Alice's mother in front of her own eyes.

For the last time Alice took out her blue contacts, revealing her true eyes—one blue, one brown. "This is who I am. This is my truth." She wiped her eyes, emotional. "I know I wasn't invited into your dreams, so please forgive me. And always know, your secrets are safe with me."

She nodded to John: she was finished.

Before he had turned off the camera, Ward stood up.

"I'm Ward Newman. I want you to know my whole truth too. I worked for Cassandra Mace for three years. Last month, she told me she had a new assignment. Most of the stuff she had asked me to do before was normal, like picking up her daughter for medical stuff. But this one was different.

"Cassandra Mace gave me a quarter of a million bucks to hire Pedro Garcia to create a viral campaign. A campaign so powerful that millions would dream about someone, remember them as if they'd known them their whole lives. The idea was based on an old marketing hoax. And if Garcia made it work, she would pay him a lot more to keep manipulating people's minds for a bigger purpose: to get her boss, Shannon, re-elected.

"Now Shannon will have a story for you, but don't believe a word he says. He was in on every detail of it. He and Cassandra are a team. They always have been."

Ward held up his phone, and John zoomed in.

"There's a subliminal message hidden there," Ward said. "It says, 'I am your whole truth.' It's subtle. Maybe you won't notice it. But trust me, it's there. And even if you don't, the fact you are thinking about the President means you are likely to dream or want to dream about him. In an insidious way, the President becomes part of your unconscious—and from all I have learned about the unconscious, what happens there doesn't stay there. It makes you act out."

The truth was finally out. The camera had captured all of it.

"Thanks for that, Alice, Ward," John said after a minute. "That's brilliant." Just as he was about to switch the camera off, Luna padded over to Ward.

Ward couldn't move. But the same dog who had snarled at him so horribly now wagged her tail, then gave a graceful stretch before him, her tail sweeping the floor.

Before Ward knew it, he was pulling Luna to him, burying his face in her soft fur. Somehow the memories of his mother's voice, her screams and accusations, came flooding back.

I am worth something. I am enough.

He stayed there, tears glistening in his eyes. The camera captured it: anyone watching could see these were not tears of sadness.

The shot of a wronged woman and a crying man with a devoted dog by their side would be hard to top.

"It's time." Max Wild jumped up from his workstation. "I'm uploading Alice's and Ward's videos now, to everywhere."

"Ready?" John asked.

"Ready," they all said in unison.

Chapter 31

"Here goes."

"What name is it all uploading under?" Alice asked.

"My own, of course. The name's Bond, John Bond."

Every damning piece of footage was uploaded, John Bond's byline out there for all the world to see, on all the different social media sites. The audacity of it floored Ward.

If this didn't ignite protests calling for Shannon's resignation, the country was more brainwashed than Ward had ever thought.

Instantly comments started popping up on X.

WTF? President Shannon commissioned a viral campaign for his re-election. That's election interference, right? Federal offense?

How is the mainstream media not covering this?

Orlando News Now *has a piece!*

Tallahassee Democrat's *running one too.*

Check the Reality *site. It's where the original story came from. Now CNN, MSNBC, even conservative outlets are running it.*

Fck off, my dreams are mine and mine alone.

The posts spread to other sites, comments flooding in over the next few hours. Most of them were supportive.

Next Max Wild called their attention to the TV.

Frank Better, a perpetually exhausted-looking news anchor who seemed to have presented the news to the world since the beginning of time, appeared onscreen.

"This is breaking news. President Shannon's communication department has issued a statement regarding the videos posted by journalist John Bond..." Better paused. "Yes, that's his real name. No relation to the real James Bond. It's coming through now."

Another pregnant pause.

"C'mon," said Griffin.

The screen flickered a little as Better held a statement from the White House. "The statement reads: 'Details are only just coming in, so stay tuned. For now, rest assured, these absurd lies about President Shannon attempting to steal the election via dream hacking, a.k.a. mind control, were orchestrated by Pedro Garcia, a psychiatrist and professor at the University of Florida. He was paid to create the viral campaign involving the strange woman who appeared in the nightmares of thousands. That strange woman was based on the profile of Alice Sinclair, an underperforming professor of psychology who was his own daughter. Evil is in her blood, as she coldheartedly murdered her father to silence him when he was about to reveal her involvement. It is believed they both worked closely with Ward Newman, who was in the President's Administration, although the President never met him. More investigation is needed, but I promise you, we will not rest until we have answers, and the corrupt individuals behind this are where they belong—behind bars. We will lock them up and throw away the key.'"

It was the very thing that Ward had feared would happen, he would become the prime scapegoat, a pawn in their twisted game. Shannon and Cassandra were framing both him and Alice as the villains in this dream game.

"Bastards." The lie might even work in their favor. Alice and Ward would be tried by public opinion and convicted, and the President would be the man of justice.

Better went on, "Cassandra Mace, the President's personal assistant and communications director for the southern states, is right now preparing to hold an emergency news conference. We're going live."

Cassandra appeared onscreen; her hair wild in the breeze. "The President has asked me to address the videos and recordings circulating on social media and the accusations leveled against the President and myself. I vehemently deny these baseless accusations. Yes, Ward Newman was my assistant, but I terminated him as soon as I learned he had been collaborating with Pedro Garcia to create the viral campaign involving the strange woman. Newman claimed it was a dry run for a similar campaign to re-elect President Shannon, and that I paid Garcia hundreds of thousands of dollars to do so. The man is deluded, and not to be trusted—he is rumored to be having an affair with the strange woman in the viral dreams. I categorically deny all of it, and any news you hear to the contrary is fake news. For further questions, speak to my lawyers."

Max snorted. "She must know that every word she's saying only makes her look more guilty. I'm going to upload the contents of Ward's phone now. It proves their involvement from the start."

He was just about to start the upload when something made him jump up. "Rooftop cams just picked this up! Two planes coming in low over the neighborhood."

"Twin-engine Cessnas, 402 and 310." Griffin studied the screen. "They're low, about 500 feet, and—shit! They're releasing something."

Alice heard the planes' engines rumbling in the distance, terrifying. She ran to the computer, watching as two planes made another pass, releasing some sort of gas that swirled through the air. It reminded her of the crop-spraying planes she'd seen in Florida. She grabbed a throw blanket from the couch and draped it over Luna's head.

Then she saw dozens of objects filling the sky above their heads, circling like vultures.

"Max, are those drones?"

"You bet." Max didn't take his eyes off the screen. "My gut told me something was going to hit the fan, so before we started uploading your video and Ward's, I called for backup. These drones are photographing everything—more evidence. It's coming to my phone now."

"Send it to me," John screamed. "I'll post it along with the live coverage I'm doing right now."

"Sending it now. Sending to everyone. They're gassing an entire street. The world must see this in real time. A neighborhood of innocent people gassed, just to make sure they get their target—us. They will blame it on extremists, as they always do."

Suddenly, there was a loud bang at the front door. Max Wild was up first, grabbing a gas mask from the cupboard, which turned out to be stocked full of them. "Everyone, grab one of these and head to the back room. Lock the doors. Don't come out."

Alice dragged Luna to the back room; the others moved quickly. Griffin pulled the curtains closed, her eyes flicking to another wide-screen TV blasting in the corner.

Frank Better was back onscreen. "We've just received live reports online, which appear to show drones over an Orlando neighborhood where twin-engine planes have inexplicably released a toxic gas." Perhaps it was an error due to crop-spraying season, he suggested. "Paramedics are heading to the site." He went on to announce the exact neighborhood where their safe house was. "If you're in the area, authorities are urging you to stay indoors. We're awaiting a statement from the White House."

The room was alive with the truth.

The next bombshell that hit was physical: Griffin unlocked the doors, three heavily armed officers entered, their gear clanking.

Alice couldn't tell if they were state or federal agents.

"We've got a cop on the roof," one of the officers said, "ready to take down those twin engines if they make another pass. Just waiting for backup." He looked at the group. "If you can use a gun, join us. If not, sit tight here."

Ward volunteered immediately, then Griffin, and the team swept out of the room. The rest of them watched the chaos unfold on the big screen, an episode of 24 that was really happening.

The roof was chaotic—guns, gear, shadows moving, waiting. The planes appeared, twin engines roaring, coming for them.

Shots rang out.

Then—*boom*. One of the planes exploded midair, flames erupting from its engine. The aircraft hurtled out of control, mercifully missing the street and crashing in the woods nearby.

They'd done it. They'd taken down the threat.

But there was no time to relax. The elite crew swept them away, headed toward a military base north of Orlando.

Next thing Alice knew, she was in a warm but windowless room. The others were there, the room filled with expensive tech, and food, fresh clothing, toiletries, and adrenaline. The FBI had everything ready for them; it was as if they had known what was going to unfold.

That night, shell-shocked, they all collapsed in their new beds.

Alice fell into a long, dreamless sleep. Luna curled up beside her, snoring loudly.

Chapter 32

Alice had never felt so hungry. The next morning at breakfast, she piled her plate high. Ward, Griffin, Max, and John also seemed ravenous, clearing their plates.

They all still hadn't processed the events of the previous days.

Alice had to pinch herself every now and then, to make sure this was reality.

A woman hurried into the kitchen. "Hi, I'm Greta," she said.

"Greta?" Alice went white. "For real?"

Alice's boss, the head of the psychology department, was standing before her.

"Yeah. Welcome to the new me," Greta said. "I'm working for the CIA now—undercover, of course. Turns out being fluent in three languages and a pillar of society *does* mean a thing. Anyway, this isn't about me. You're all safe here, and everything can come into the light." She touched a remote on a nearby table, and a screen on the wall sprang into life, projecting images: Shannon shackled and escorted out of the White House. Then Cassandra, taken into custody in Florida.

Alice felt a flicker of hope for them, for the country, for the world. Perhaps telling the truth, the whole truth, could really set everyone free.

Then TV host Frank appeared on the screen, the circles under his eyes even darker than usual. "This is lack of sleep talking, but after this night of madness, I have a message for Alice Sinclair: there's going to be a vacancy in the Oval Office. Alice Sinclair has exposed the government and all its corruption, and she's paid a steep penalty. We know her now: she's courageous, she's kind, she's clever. She's now the most famous woman in the world. Above all, she's honest—and aren't we all eager for a slice of that? Alice, if you're watching, what do you say?

Will you run? You're probably thinking to yourself, *No, it's not possible*, but why not? No more impossible than a movie or reality TV star? Maybe you're struggling with the ethics too, because you've been inside people's heads. But look, you didn't ask for this to happen to you, and you can't change the past. Some are born great. Others have greatness thrust upon them. What do you say, Alice Sinclair? Will you now truly become the woman of our dreams?"

Alice sat frozen.

What do you think? Ward mouthed silently.

She hadn't asked for any of this. But here she was.

What if she could use her unwelcome fame for good? Their conflicted world urgently needed authenticity and something better.

The irony of Frank Better as the good messenger was not lost on her.

But was a better future something *she* could offer? Was she enough?

Luna padded over, nudging Alice's leg. *I'm with you.*

Alice stroked her dog's head. "What's the worst thing that could happen?"

Luna's tail circled like a helicopter blade.

Alice turned to Ward. *I think yes.*

"Hey, everyone!" Ward said. "Alice has an announcement!"

Chapter 33

Alice spent most of Election Day at her campaign headquarters in downtown Orlando. Her entire Night Born team had gathered; only Ward was missing, busy caring for his wife and 2-day-old newborn son at home.

The campaign space was charged and buzzing. Three large televisions filled the walls, tuned to different stations, broadcasting the unfolding election results as the poll numbers began rolling in.

The pollsters had her opponent up by 10 points in Florida. Now that Shannon had been impeached by his own party and was awaiting trial, the Vice President was running against her. A smooth-talking Southern boy from New Orleans, he was charming on the surface but undeniably rotten beneath, almost as vile and corrupt as Shannon had been.

But Alice had learned not to trust the polls. Over the past grueling months of campaigning, she'd seen firsthand how misleading those numbers could be.

Alice's campaign was built on a sea-change, a belief that it was time to shine light amidst the hatred and divisiveness that still festered in too many corners of the country. The time was overdue for a change to unity, compassion, optimism.

Somehow, they had swiftly and mysteriously raised tens of millions—enough to build a powerhouse team: Joe as her campaign advisor, Amira and John as communications directors, the Grangers leading fundraising, Neal handling campaign graphics, Greta as campaign manager, Chico and Matt security, and Ward coordinating operations in the field. Griffin was now her invaluable legal counsel; she'd left the CIA to serve as Alice's ally.

Nationwide, women's organizations had rallied behind Alice, mobilizing thousands of volunteers in every corner of the country. The voices of hatred, remnants of Shannon's toxic legacy, were still there, but they seemed more isolated, quieter.

The tides were shifting.

Her campaign wasn't just about winning votes, though; at its heart was a bold new educational grassroots initiative, the Department of Visionary Expertise: DOVE. The plan was for dreamwork, intuition training, meditation, and personal growth tools to be integrated and pioneered in schools, universities, hospitals, offices, community and education centers across the nation. Alice had once dreamed of publishing a book to promote these ideas. Now, if she won, she'd have the chance to turn them into policy—a vision so ambitious it barely seemed real.

Tonight, all they could do was wait.

Someone had ordered pizza for everyone, and the boxes of happiness soon arrived in a steady stream of heat, the unmistakable aroma of melted cheese filling the air.

Chico and Matt checked the two delivery men thoroughly. One of them, a lanky guy with a name tag that read "Jacob from Jake's Pizzeria," stopped when he saw Alice.

"I... I dreamed about you months ago," he stammered. "The dream felt so real that when I woke up, I had to ask myself if I'd been dreaming at all."

These exchanges still happened with surreal frequency. Alice asked her usual question: "And what was I doing in your dream?"

He set several pizza boxes down on the nearest table, hands trembling as he opened the top one. "You were doing this." He gestured toward the contents—vegetarian pizza, pepperoni, and a pizza piled high with every topping. "Serving pizza. Just like this."

"Serving?"

Jacob nodded, pulling a stack of paper plates from his bag. "Which one would you like?"

"One of each," she said.

Jacob plated her slices, quick and efficient. Alice plucked a slice of chicken and a piece of salami, slipping them to Luna.

Then she turned back to Jacob. "Was my dog in your dream?"

"She was," he replied. "Her name's Luna, right? In the dream, you called her by her name."

"You're the first person to tell me that. That Luna was in the dream with me."

It dawned on Alice: Luna, named for the moon, a symbol of intuition and the growth born from the mysteries of the night, wasn't just her dog. She was Alice's heart and soul. The very spirit of the Night Born. A force of unconditional love and kindness, a quiet reminder to the team of what truly mattered.

Luna had no specific role, no grand part in the unfolding drama. Her role was simply to be there, steadfast, walking beside them through every challenge. She was a symbol of balance, reminding them to never let their work or their cause overshadow their connection to the world, to savor the small joys, and take time to "smell the roses."

Alice reminded herself that her own middle name was Rose: a sign, a constant reminder that the journey, not the destination, was life's true adventure. It wasn't necessarily acts of great power and influential people that could fight the forces of darkness; it was the everyday acts of kindness and love among ordinary people that would ensure that there would always be a light at the end of the tunnel.

Jacob's voice broke into her reverie. "I pray you're going to save us from ourselves. A second term of Shannon's policies would be disastrous. The first term was just a dry run. They've learned the ropes now, refined their machine. I'm scared, really scared, of what will happen if they win again."

"Please don't be scared, Jacob," Alice reassured. "Fear gives what you are scared of power." No need to sift through Jungian theories; this clarity was hers now, ready to share with anyone who would listen.

"Remember this: you are so much stronger than you realize. Never give up on yourself, or on the people and things you love. Whatever happens, you have the power within you to transform fear into strength, to turn pain into purpose. And Jacob, look up the meaning of your name. It means 'to dream.' I have no doubt that you can do just about anything when you dare to believe in the future of your dreams."

"But what if darkness wins again? How am I going to be able to still love my fellow Americans if they make this happen?"

"You'll find a way," Alice asserted. "You'll grieve. You'll take the time to reflect and learn from your mistakes, what you might have done, and still can do, better. And then you'll take a deep breath, regroup, and course correct. That's what strong people do. Their scars become their teachers. The more scars you carry, the wiser you become."

"Hmm, you're saying that no matter what happens, there's always hope for us?"

"You already know that. Your intuition knows it to be true. You just need to start trusting it. Stop looking for answers in the crowd and start following your own inner compass. *Inside out.* Make that your mantra. And don't ever stop asking questions. What if is the fuel that pushes humanity forward."

Joe approached, waiting on the sidelines. Then his stomach growled.

"Sir? I hear you loud and clear. Vegetarian, pepperoni, or the works?"

He nodded toward the second delivery guy, who was busy handing out slices from even more boxes. "Or cheese pizza and cheese with broccoli and mushrooms."

"Vegetarian," Joe reached for a plate.

"Was Joe in your dream, too?" Alice asked the young man.

Jacob shook his head. "No, ma'am. Just you and Luna."

Joe had an announcement. "The polls in four swing states have closed," he told the room. "Votes are being counted, but early signs show Alice is ahead in all of them."

Alice kept her face neutral. Nothing would be certain until every poll closed, and the swing states started revealing their hand. "Let's hope it holds."

"It will," Jacob said.

The other delivery guy walked over. "Paul, this is Alice Sinclair—our next President."

Paul's face lit up. "I'm psyched to meet you, ma'am. I saw your interview on TV. Loved listening to someone who's clearly sane for a change." He turned to Joe. "And Mr. Sebastian, your books are my go-to source of spiritual guidance. You helped me so much when my dad died, you helped make sense of it all and that I can still talk to him in my heart. If you know what I mean."

Sane? Nobody had ever called Alice that before. Right now, she felt anything but—insane with anxiety, her mind spinning with possibilities.

What would happen if she didn't win? She had no immediate plan, beyond retreating to her teaching, maybe finally writing her long-delayed debut book on true dream power. If anyone would still publish it.

Joe seized the moment, "Let's take Luna for a walk." The dog's ears perked up at the magic word.

The three of them slipped out the back, Alice's Secret Service detail trailing at a respectful distance. Even after months of campaigning, Alice still hadn't quite adjusted to their presence.

They walked slowly toward the garden behind the building, the path lit by soft, moon-shaped lights. Luna stopped at the fountain, lapping at the water. Alice and Joe sat on the fountain's edge.

"We haven't really talked about us if you win," Joe said.

"You'll be my presidential advisor."

"No, I mean us. On a personal level. Should we get married? Isn't that the respectable thing to do? Besides, your intuitive senses are waking up. You may not admit it yet, but you're a natural-born psychic. I'd love to mentor you—make us a team. Alice and Joe: the woman of everyone's dreams and her Joseph. Jacob's favorite son. The dreamer with the colorful coat who interpreted Pharaoh's dreams."

Alice put a finger over his lips. "Being respectable isn't a good reason to get married."

"Love is," he said.

"Is that what you feel?" Alice put her hand on his cheek, soft. "I'm so grateful to you, Joe," she took a step back from him, "but I'm not ready to become your echo. Maybe one day that will change. I mean, if this year has taught me anything, it's that nothing stays the same. But right now, I can't follow anyone, not even you. Not even the almighty Jung.

"You once asked me what I believe in. I finally have the answer. I must believe in myself. I need to discover my own vision for a better world. People have seen me in their dreams before I have seen myself. For far too long, I've hidden behind the advice and theories of others—behind these *bloody* blue lenses. That stops now. I need to—" she searched for the word, "I need to complete myself."

Alice reached into her pocket and took out her lens case, holding the blue lenses between her fingers. Then she crushed them. She held Joe's gaze, unflinching.

"You mentioned the power of names," she said. "Only recently did it hit me—what Alice truly means. 'A source of light.' Don't you see? My purpose has been there all along, hidden in my dreams, etched in plain sight with my very own name. I've become, quite literally, the embodiment of the American dream. A small light of hope for everyone in the darkness. Proof that anything is possible when you believe in your dreams and follow your conscience. Every person—no matter their background or issues—has the freedom and power to rise, to create a better life. I..."

"I get it," he said. "You need to be free—to become the best, truest version of yourself. In doing that, you free me to do the same for myself. That's unconditional love, Alice. The kind that doesn't bind; it liberates. Just know I'll be here if you ever need—or want—me. We don't have to just gaze into each other's eyes, you know. We can look up at the stars together, at the same horizon."

"We have time to figure all this out," Alice said. "The results aren't even in yet. After all, if I lose... maybe I'll vanish into blissful solitude and academic obscurities. I can see it now: back to dusty libraries, forcing my unread books on poor students."

Joe raised his fist. "Here's to whatever comes next."

They bumped knuckles, sealing a silent pact.

"The results," Joe declared. "They're coming in early. I can feel it."

"How early?"

"In—" Joe began, but the back door slammed open as cheers erupted from inside. The campaign team flooded into the garden.

"You won! President-Elect Professor Alice Sinclair!"

"Three hundred thirteen electoral votes!"

"Ninety-two million in the popular vote!"

Luna howled, caught up in the whirlwind of emotion. The group enveloped Alice and Joe, hugging, laughing, a cacophony of joy.

Then Alice stopped breathing. Her eyes, wide open, caught a glimpse of something unseen in the doorway.

Her mother stood there, just for an instant. Radiant, proud, and unmistakable.

Thank you, Mom.

The grainy figure faded into the shadows. *Now go and govern the free world,* her message from the unseen world of dreams was clear. The world needed a leader born not from ambition, but from purpose, of need, ready to carry the weight of a nation's dreams into the uncharted future.

And watching the election unfold on a big TV screen with Rachel resting her head on his shoulder and his baby son, Jacob, cradled in his arms, Ward let out a cheer.

And then he closed his eyes. Behind them he saw Alice holding his hand in the backseat of a speeding car. He held the dream tenderly there for a while, then opened his eyes, kissing the smooth forehead of his newborn.

Epilogue

Florida, USA

Alice lay in bed for what seemed like forever, wondering if tonight's dreams would bring more revelations.

In the early hours of the morning, she woke with a start, but the sole remnant of her dreams was a tired recurring cliché: her teeth falling out as she stood in her bathroom trying to put her blue lenses in.

Not again. Once more she tried every mental trick to dig deeper, scanning her body and mind for hidden dream details — but the image of her teeth falling out wouldn't budge from her mental inbox. It was as mundane as it was maddening. The same old anxiety dream. Classic. Predictable. And entirely unwelcome. The disappointment of it all almost tempted her to dismiss it entirely, to roll over and forget.

But then something deep inside stirred — a whisper, a nudge. She wouldn't cast the recurring dream aside; it was happening for a reason.

She sat up, switched on her nightlight, and opened her *Red Dream* book. She scribbled the details, yawning as she wrote.

It wasn't until she set the pen down that the meaning began to crystallize. Her entire life, she'd felt toothless. The blue lenses she wore daily masked her eyes, dulling her identity, muting her originality. Those lenses — like the falling teeth — symbolized her drive to conform, to fit neatly into the world's expectations.

But no more. Her eyes weren't a curse to be hidden. They were a truth to be embraced. They were the raw, unfiltered windows to her soul.

Whatever discomfort they stirred in others wasn't her burden to carry.

Euphoria washed over her. It wasn't just her eyes she needed to free: it was herself. The fear of standing out, of being seen for who she truly was, had held her back long enough. For the first time since she was a child, Alice dared to dream without boundaries.

Her world wasn't just shifting, it was opening, and she was ready to leap through. Her pen raced across the pages of her dream journal, possessed by a force she couldn't control. It felt alive in her hand, guided by something far greater than her conscious mind. Memories poured out, vivid and urgent, as if ripped straight from some hidden archive of her soul.

Alice, standing in a surreal dreamland, its edges as clear to her now as reality. Alice, a phantom in millions of other people's dreams, her face etched into the unconscious of a nation, the world. Alice, evading the relentless pursuit of the Secret Service, vanishing into shadows and secrecy. Alice, bonded with Luna, her angelic black dog, a silent guardian of her journey. Alice dancing with Ward and walking with Joe. Alice, forging the Night Born—a league of visionaries using intuition, creativity, and empathy to dismantle corruption and overturn a sordid re-election campaign. Alice, saying a final goodbye to her parents and exorcising the twisted shadows of her past. *Alice standing before a crowd of millions, taking the oath of President of the United States, a twin symbol of hope and rebellion.*

The memories, so vivid, so intensely felt, she had to pinch herself. Was this for real? She resisted the compulsion to make herself blink as a reality check; she wanted to stay in this moment, to truly capture and feel it without breaking the spell. She wouldn't force the blinking but let it come naturally when it would. For once, let life and the power of now flow.

For a few precious, fragile seconds, it didn't matter if what she recalled had truly happened or if she was still dreaming. It didn't matter if she was Alice dreaming of being the President Elect, or the President Elect dreaming she was Alice. The boundary between reality and dream blurred into irrelevance.

For the first time, she believed both could be real. Both could be true.

As the first light of dawn crept through her window and the birds began to sing, a profound calm settled over her. She had never felt so truly, madly, deeply alive, so electrified, so empowered from the inside out. Whatever lay ahead, she had already unlocked the greatest power of all: unshakable faith in the beauty of her dreams, whether seen with her eyes wide open or wide shut.

Not the End!

My dear visionary readers, thank you for your time—an irreplaceable gift. Whether you realized it or not, as your eyes blinked and tracked these words, you opened a doorway. The idea that your nocturnal dreams hold meaning, power, and influence in your waking life has quietly slipped into your subconscious. Trust that inner spark. Follow it.

Tomorrow, or perhaps in the coming days, you might wake with a startlingly vivid dream etched in your mind. Don't dismiss it. Where your conscious attention flows during the day, your unconscious mind mirrors at night, crafting symbols and metaphors to guide you. The boundaries between waking life and dreams are thinner than most dare to believe. Déjà-rêvé, gut instincts, synchronicities—they are all echoes of your dreaming mind breaking through into waking hours.

It is a truth universally unacknowledged that when you dream, you don't become someone else. You're still you, exploring a different realm of consciousness. Your brain, relentless and alive, nudges you to dream bigger, to push past limits, every single moment of your existence. Whether you like it or loathe it, we are all dreaming beings having a human experience. Dreaming unites us all.

And so, as we part ways and you step into your next great adventure, I won't wish you sweet dreams. As my story has shown, comfort doesn't teach. If there's one enduring truth I've learned, it's that growth lies beyond the boundaries of safety. The human spirit thrives not by circling the same paths but by spiralling upward, evolving with every fear faced and every lesson learned, to view what was from a higher and higher perspective. To wake up to yourself every morning with greater wisdom and higher love—that is your purpose.

Meaning isn't found in external validations or in dancing to the expectations of others, but in the hidden landscapes within yourself. What lies beneath your surface, beneath everyone's surface, is where the real magic is found—raw, untamed, and transformative. So, my dearest visionary readers, until our paths cross again, whether in waking life or the quiet depths of a dream, I leave you with this: embrace the unexpected. Decode the strange. Look beneath the surface for deeper meaning and the invisible strings of love always. Revel in your gloriously unexpected adventure. And never ever forget that the best and most beautiful things are unseen. They cannot be seen or even touched. To quote the immortal Helen Keller, they must be felt with the heart, that is why we close our eyes when we cry, kiss, and dream.

Now go to sleep and wake up. Because if my unexpected adventure has proven anything, it's that the greatest power you hold lies in your ability to dream and be born anew every single day and every precious night.

Professor Alice Rose Sinclair, Nobel Peace Prize, 2033

All that we see or seem is but a dream within a dream.

—*Edgar Allan Poe*

Recent Bestsellers from 6th Books Are:

The Scars of Eden
Paul Wallis
How do we distinguish between our ancestors' ideas of
God and close encounters of an extraterrestrial kind?
Paperback: 978-1-78904-852-0 ebook: 978-1-78904-853-7

The Afterlife Unveiled
Stafford Betty
What the dead are telling us about their world!
What happens after we die? Spirits speaking through
mediums know, and they want us to know.
This book unveils their world...
Paperback: 978-1-84694-496-3 ebook: 978-1-84694-926-5

Harvest: The True Story of Alien Abduction
G.L. Davies
G.L. Davies's most-terrifying investigation yet reveals one
woman's terrifying ordeal of alien visitation, nightmarish
visions and a prophecy of destruction on a scale never
before seen in Pembrokeshire's peaceful history.
Paperback: 978-1-78904-385-3 ebook: 978-1-78904-386-0

M.E. Myself and I - Diary of a Psychic
Nicky Alan
A brutally honest journey showing strength of the human
spirit, faith in the unseen and a tenacious will to survive.
Paperback: 978-1-78904-451-5 ebook: 978-1-78904-452-2

Phantoms of Christmas Past
Paul Weatherhead
True stories of seasonal ghost hoaxes and strange phantom panics from the nineteenth and early twentieth centuries.
Paperback: 978-1-80341-840-7 ebook: 978-1-80341-866-7

Spirit Release
Sue Allen
A guide to psychic attack, curses, witchcraft, spirit attachment, possession, soul retrieval, haunting, deliverance, exorcism and more, as taught at the College of Psychic Studies.
Paperback: 978-1-84694-033-0 ebook: 978-1-84694-651-6

Advanced Psychic Development
Becky Walsh
Learn how to practise as a professional, contemporary spiritual medium.
Paperback: 978-1-84694-062-0 ebook: 978-1-78099-941-8

Where After
Mariel Forde Clarke
A journey that will compel readers to view life after death in a completely different way.
Paperback: 978-1-78904-617-5 ebook: 978-1-78904-618-2

Paranormal Perspectives:
One Big Box of 'Paranormal Tricks'?
John Fraser
Think Zen and the Art of Spending the Night in a Haunted House, a celebration of the dream of finding something undiscovered and different.
Paperback: 978-1-80341-524-6 ebook: 978-1-80341-532-1

Haunted: Horror of Haverfordwest
G.L. Davies
Blissful beginnings for a young couple turn into a nightmare after purchasing their dream home in Wales in 1989.
Paperback: 978-1-78535-843-2 ebook: 978-1-78535-844-9

Astral Projection Made Easy
and overcoming the fear of death
Stephanie June Sorrell
From the popular Made Easy series, Astral Projection Made Easy helps to eliminate the fear of death through discussion of life beyond the physical body.
Paperback: 978-1-84694-611-0 ebook: 978-1-78099-225-9

Developing Your Supernatural Awareness
Fredrick Woodard
The common themes and details pointed out in this book will develop or enhance your understanding of our supernatural awareness and connection with our interactive universe.
Paperback: 978-1-80341-478-2 ebook: 978-1-80341-479-9

Readers of ebooks can buy or view any of these bestsellers by clicking on the live link in the title. Most titles are published in paperback and as an ebook. Paperbacks are available in traditional bookshops. Both print and ebook formats are available online.

Find more titles and sign up to our readers' newsletter at
www.6th-books.com

Join the 6th books Facebook group at
6th Books The world of the Paranormal